*This copy of*

TH................................RY

belong.........

# The
# Sierra Gold Mystery

## Carolyn Keene

SPARROW
BOOKS

A Sparrow Book
Published by Arrow Books Limited
17–21 Conway Street, London W1P 6JD

An imprint of the Hutchinson Publishing Group

London Melbourne Sydney Auckland
Johannesburg and agencies
throughout the world

First published in Great Britain 1983

Made and printed in Great Britain
by The Anchor Press Ltd
Tiptree, Essex

ISBN 0 09 930890 8

# CONTENTS

*The author extends sincere appreciation to the following persons and organizations for their valuable help in her research of historical data used in this fictional story: Muriel Thebaut, William Wintle, Frank L. Fish, Frank Foisie, Jack Foisie, the Bancroft Library at Berkeley, California, and the Amador County, California, Chamber of Commerce.*

*Mrs. Thebaut, Mr. Wintle, and Mr. Fish have kindly consented to the use of their names in this book.*

CHAPTER I

# A Stolen Gift

"THERE'S San Francisco! Isn't it exciting to be back in the United States again!" Louise Dana exclaimed. The pretty, dark-haired girl was seated beside her sister Jean in a jet plane just arriving from Honolulu. They were returning from an early November trip to Bangkok.

"And with a new mystery to solve!" Blond, vivacious Jean pressed her face against the window to see the outskirts of the attractive city. "I suppose San Francisco could be called the city of gold."

Her sister agreed. "It certainly could—what with all the gold dug during the eighteen-fifties and sixties in the Sierras and brought here."

Jean nodded, then said, "I'm glad Starhurst School has postponed opening because of the fire. That will give us time to work on Aunt Carol's mystery."

"Yes," Louise agreed. "And isn't it wonderful the school is adding a junior college! It means, when we graduate from the lower school, we can stay there longer with our friends."

Louise, seventeen, and Jean, a year younger, were students at Starhurst School for girls in Penfield.

"That'll be nice," Jean remarked. "Louise, what do you suppose Aunt Carol's mystery is?"

"Maybe she has lost something like a ring or a bracelet and wants us to find it."

"Possibly, but that sounds too easy," Jean said jokingly. Then, with dancing eyes, she speculated, "Aunt Carol may have learned there's a secret room or stairway in her house but can't locate it."

"Whatever it is, the mystery must be very important," said Louise. "After all, Aunt Carol phoned Uncle Ned in New York to wire us in Honolulu that we must come to Sacramento as soon as we reached California."

Jean laughed. "Just lead us to Aunt Carol's!" she said, snapping her fingers. "You and I are ripe for another mystery, no matter how tough!"

The two girls were interrupted by their Aunt Harriet, who sat across the aisle.

"Janet has something to tell you," Miss Dana said. The sweet-faced woman was referring to a very pretty girl of eighteen, Janet Crane, seated beside her. Janet had been on a Hawaiian trip with a tourist group. While in Honolulu she and the Danas had met and become friends.

Janet, who lived in San Francisco, smiled and leaned toward Louise and Jean. "I *must* see you all again soon. Suppose I call you for a date?"

"That sounds wonderful," said Louise. "We'd love to, but we're heading for Sacramento."

"I know," said Janet, "but you probably won't be going there for a couple of days. You'll want to do some sightseeing in San Francisco before you leave."

As Janet spoke, the plane set down on the runway. It sped along for a short distance, then slowed down and taxied to the terminal building.

The passengers unfastened their seat belts and reached for their hats, coats, and hand luggage. Each of the Danas carried a small overnight bag which she had used as a footrest during the flight.

Minutes later, Miss Dana and her nieces were saying good-by to Janet Crane in the waiting room and promising to see their new friend before leaving San Francisco if possible. "We're going to phone Aunt Carol as soon as we get to the hotel," Louise added. "Then we'll know how long we can stay here."

"Don't fail me," Janet said, laughing.

As soon as the Danas had claimed their larger pieces of luggage, a porter found a taxi for them and they set off for the hotel.

"Janet's a wonderful girl," said Jean. "I wish she didn't live so far away from where we do."

Aunt Harriet smiled. "With jet travel, home doesn't seem so far away any more. Just the same, I'll be glad to get back so I can see my brother Ned when his ship docks."

Uncle Ned Dana was captain of the Atlantic ocean liner *Balaska*. It was only when his ship docked in New York that he was able to come to Oak Falls, where he and Aunt Harriet had a home which they shared with their orphaned nieces.

"We'll have to solve our mystery fast," Jean said with a laugh.

The taxi drew up to the hotel entrance and two porters came out to assist with the luggage. After Miss Dana had registered, the three travellers were shown to two adjoining bedrooms on an upper floor.

"We'll have to start worrying about time again." Miss Dana sighed and glanced at the clock on the radio-television console in the girls' room. As she adjusted the hands of her wrist watch, she said slowly, "In San Francisco it's exactly ten A.M. In Honolulu it's—"

"Oh, please," Jean begged. "I was always mixed up on time on our trip to Bangkok. I don't want to think about all the hours of sleep we're losing going East!"

Louise set her overnight bag on one of the twin beds. She took a key from her purse and opened the bag. Among her personal belongings Louise had packed several small gifts and souvenirs which she had purchased in Bangkok.

Her most prized possession was a beautiful star sapphire ring. It had been given to her by Malee Wongsuwan in Thailand as a token of gratitude for solving the baffling *Mystery of the Bamboo Bird*. Ever since their first case, *Mystery of the Stone Tiger*, Louise and Jean had been successful in finding the solutions to several mysteries.

Suddenly a strange look came over Louise's face. Quickly she began to take everything out of the overnight bag.

"Aunt Harriet! Jean!" she cried out in distress. "My lovely sapphire ring is missing!"

"Oh, no! It can't be!" Jean and her aunt cried simultaneously.

Instantly they helped Louise search, but finally had to agree with her that the ring and its handsome velvet box were gone.

"Oh, Louise!" Jean said in dismay. "This is dreadful!"

Aunt Harriet put an arm about her niece's shoulders. "Think hard, dear. When did you last have the ring? Perhaps you put it somewhere else —in your handbag or in your large suitcase."

"I know I didn't," Louise replied. But to satisfy the others she went through the suitcase and handbag. The ring was not in either of them.

The three Danas sank into the chairs, dumfounded. For several seconds none of them spoke. Then Jean exclaimed, "I might have a clue!"

She said that when Aunt Harriet, Louise, and Janet Crane had walked to the lounge, she had taken a nap in her seat by the window. When she awakened, there was a man seated alongside her.

"He was very talkative and—well, a big nuisance. He said he had been waiting for a chance to come and speak to me. Then he began to talk about Thailand. He knew we had been there and wanted to know how we liked it."

Jean went on to say that she had been coolly polite, and very general in her remarks. "He bored me with stories of his wealth and the fact that he didn't have to work."

"Hmm. Do you think he might be the 'gentleman thief' type?" Louise interrupted.

"I sure do," her sister said. "He could have opened Louise's bag while I was asleep and fished out that velvet box with the ring in it. It was unlocked."

"Yes," Louise agreed, "and since he didn't take anything else, he must have overheard me say that the star sapphire ring was the most valuable thing I was carrying."

Aunt Harriet said she thought Jean's hunch was worth investigating. "We should notify the police. They can get in touch with the airline and obtain his name." Miss Dana herself went to the telephone and put in the call.

Ten minutes later two detectives came up and questioned the girls and their aunt. The plain-clothes men agreed that Jean's reasoning was logical. One of them called the airline at once and explained why he wanted to know the name of the passenger. With Jean's full description of him, identification was easy.

The detective put down the phone and turned to the Danas. "The man's name is Basil Tripley and he gave New York City as his address."

The officers promised to work on the case immediately. Louise explained that the Danas would be in town that day at least and would let the police know when they left for Sacramento. The detectives said good-by and went off.

"Let's all keep our fingers crossed," said Jean, trying to bolster Louise's spirits. "Maybe Basil Tripley will be caught and you'll have your ring back by tonight, Sis."

Before Louise could make any comment, the telephone rang. She answered it. "Janet! How good to hear from you!"

Janet's voice did not sound natural. She was no longer the lighthearted, laughing girl with whom the Danas had been spending time the past few days.

Half sobbing, she said, "Oh, Louise, something dreadful has happened! My darling grandfather, Major Williams, whom I told you about, has disappeared! You and Jean simply must stay here and help me find him!"

## CHAPTER II

# Ancient Giants

"YOUR grandfather is missing!" Louise repeated. "Do you mean he wandered away, or has been abducted?"

"We have no idea." Janet's voice trembled. "A couple of months ago he was very ill in the hospital. Then he went to a rest home. You see, the Major lives with Mother and me. There were just the three of us. My father passed away several years ago."

Janet went on to say that Major Williams, Mrs. Crane's father, was retired from the Army. Janet had always affectionately called him "Major."

"I was on the Hawaiian trip and Mother had to go to New York on business the day after my grandfather was released from the hospital. That's why he went to the rest home. Just before Mother got back home, the Major disappeared. The police and Missing Persons Bureau have been looking for him ever since, but haven't picked up a single clue. Oh, Louise, you and Jean *will* help us find him, won't you?"

"It's a great challenge, Janet," said Louise. "I'm dreadfully sorry to hear about your grandfather. But we've promised to solve a mystery for my aunt in Sacramento. And we'll have to go back to school in two or three weeks."

Janet sighed. "Well, please do one thing for Mother and me," she said. "Please come out and have luncheon with us today and talk the matter over. I'm sure Mother will feel better just to meet you and to know that you will help us if you can."

Louise turned to her aunt and Jean, and quickly briefed them on the conversation. They accepted the luncheon invitation. Janet was delighted and set the hour for twelve-thirty. "You have my address," she said.

"Yes," Louise replied. "Keep your chin up, Janet. We'll be seeing you!"

When they reached the Crane home, Janet's mother greeted them at the front door. She was a charming woman, about forty-five, slender and attractive. But when she was not smiling, lines of worry showed on her face. During luncheon she directed the conversation to the trips the Danas and her daughter had taken. It was not until they left the table and were seated in the living room that she brought up the subject of her father.

"I kept the news from Janet for nearly a month, feeling sure that he would return, but now I must admit to a dreadful premonition that something has happened to him."

"Try not to have such thoughts, Mrs. Crane," Aunt Harriet said soothingly. "You must never give up hope."

"I've tried not to," Janet's mother said bravely, "but it has been hard. I'm sure the police and the Missing Persons Bureau have made every effort to find the Major. When Janet mentioned that you Dana girls have solved many unusual mysteries, I took fresh hope. But I realize that this is asking a great deal of you and that you already have plans to solve another mystery."

Louise and Jean looked at each other, then at their Aunt Harriet. Miss Dana smiled and gave a slight nod. "Mrs. Crane," she said, "I'm sure that if Louise and Jean did not try to assist you, at least for a short time, they would never forgive themselves—nor would I have a clear conscience."

Janet almost jumped from her chair. "You mean you'll help us find the Major? Oh, this is wonderful! I know you'll succeed!"

Louise requested Mrs. Crane to tell them all that the police and Missing Persons Bureau had already done, so there would be no unnecessary duplication in the girls' efforts. The sisters learned that all railroad, airline, steamship, and bus companies had been contacted, as well as the automobile agencies, but these had furnished no clues. Mrs. Crane said that a full description of the Major had been sent to police authorities throughout the continental United States, Canada, and Mexico.

"Of course the police conducted a local search?" Jean queried.

"Oh, yes. Every hospital, hotel, motel, and nursing home was contacted."

"How old is your father?" Louise asked Mrs. Crane.

"Seventy-five. Up to the time of the severe illness which sent him to the hospital, he was remarkably well and strong. But his doctors feel that he had not recuperated enough to have been able to go any distance from the rest home without assistance. And then there's another very important factor: My father had no money with him, so he could not have travelled far on his own."

Aunt Harriet inquired diplomatically if there were some reason Major Williams might not have wished to come back home.

Mrs. Crane looked shocked. "Why, goodness no! We were a very happy little family here."

Louise asked to see a photograph of Major Williams. Mrs. Crane brought out one taken before his illness and showed it to the Danas. The Major, they saw, was a tall, well-built man with white hair. He was smooth shaven, and had twinkling eyes.

"It certainly would not be hard to spot your father," said Jean. "He looks like just the kind of grandfather I'd like to have."

Janet and her mother smiled, then Janet said, "How will you start solving the mystery?"

"By going to the rest home and questioning a few people," Louise replied. "I realize the police were there, but perhaps by now some other information will be available."

Mrs. Crane said her father had been a patient at the Grandview Nursing Home and gave the girls the address.

Louise glanced at her watch. "Jean, why don't you and I run over to the nursing home now?"

Jean was enthusiastic. Smiling, she said, "What's holding us up? Every minute counts!"

Janet called a taxi, then the Danas said good-by to her and Mrs. Crane, and promised to do all they could to help find Major Williams.

In the taxi, later, Aunt Harriet spoke up. "I think I'll go right back to the hotel. You don't need me in your sleuthing, and I must confess I feel quite weary."

The driver was instructed to stop at the hotel. After Aunt Harriet alighted, Louise and Jean went on to the Grandview Nursing Home. It was a large, old-fashioned house, pleasantly situated on a hill overlooking the bay. The house was surrounded by an attractive garden.

Louise paid the taxi driver, while Jean opened the iron gate to a concrete walk leading to the office. The sisters found a businesslike nurse on duty. She asked whom they wished to see.

Quickly Louise explained the girls' mission. The woman frowned. "I have given out information about Major Williams to the police and other authorities," she stated curtly. "It is an imposition to be asked to do so again."

The sisters knew it was useless to pursue the subject with this uncooperative person. Jean merely said, "I see."

Suddenly the nurse seemed to relent. "Look around, if you wish. Maybe one of the patients can help you."

Louise and Jean peered into the large living room. Several elderly men and women sat about watching a television show. One of the women smiled up at the girls, so Louise went forward and sat down beside her.

"Did you know Major Williams while he was staying here?" she asked.

"Yes, indeed. A fine man."

"Where was his room?" Jean asked.

"At the end of the hall on this floor," the woman replied. "The nurse in charge there is Miss Spring. She'll show you."

The Danas walked down the corridor, glancing casually into the various bedrooms. Presently they saw a nurse and asked if she were Miss Spring.

"Yes, I am," the nurse said, smiling. "May I help you?"

Louise explained why she and Jean had come. "I know the police have questioned all of you thoroughly, but would you mind answering some questions for us? We'd appreciate it."

"Not at all," Miss Spring replied. "To tell you the truth, I'll feel really relieved when they find Major Williams. I wasn't on duty at the time he disappeared, but I feel sorry for the nurse who was. Naturally she blames herself."

Louise asked what Major Williams liked to do most while he was at Grandview. Miss Spring thought for a moment, then said, "Well, he was a great reader. He always had a lot of books in his room, and he used to go to our small library a good deal."

"Did he leave his own books here?"

"Oh, yes. They've been taken to the library."

Louise said the girls would go to look at them, then asked, "Have you formed any personal opinion as to why Major Williams disappeared?"

Miss Spring looked around to make sure no one else was listening. "I haven't told this to a soul, not even the police," she said in a whisper. "But I have a strong hunch that Major Williams ran away because he thought he was going to have to live here the rest of his life."

"Why, I thought he was going back home with his daughter and granddaughter," Jean said in amazement.

"That's what all of us here thought," Miss Spring answered. "But I used to hear Major Williams mumbling in his sleep during his nap time. Once I heard him say he didn't want to stay in a nursing home for the rest of his life, and felt bad that he was no longer wanted."

"How sad!" Louise murmured. She asked if Miss Spring could go with them to the library and point out the books which Major Williams either owned or had borrowed.

"I'll be glad to." The nurse led Jean and Louise to the small room where bookshelves lined the walls.

Major Williams' personal volumes proved to be current fiction. But those he had borrowed from the library were on two different subjects. One volume was a history of California. In this, he had inserted slips of paper to set off a chapter on Gold Rush days.

"Thank you, Miss Spring. Don't let us detain you," said Louise, and the nurse went off.

The Danas turned their attention to the other volume Major Williams had borrowed.

"The story of the lost continent of Mu in the Pacific Ocean," Louise observed as she and Jean scanned the pages. "Sounds fantastic!"

Jean nodded. "What an amazing catastrophe! It

says here that fire arose out of the centre of the continent and the whole land mass sank under water—except the part now known as Easter Island. It must have been a gigantic earthquake."

"And look what it says here," Louise said excitedly. "A race of giants lived on Mu. Scientists now call them the Lemurians. They practiced a very high culture. What a pity that they and their civilization were lost!"

"Here's something interesting," Jean spoke up. "Scientists infer that the Lemurians were great navigators, and some of them came to California and discovered gold!"

When the Danas found a paragraph which had been marked in pencil on the side, Jean asked, "Do you suppose Major Williams did this?"

"It's possible."

The paragraph told of a legend that the Lemurians had secreted a great horde of gold or golden objects in a California cave. Its location was assumed to be in the area of the Sierra Nevada mountain range.

Louise and Jean looked at each other, the same thought running through their minds. Had Major Williams gone adventuring in the gold country?

"Considering the section the Major marked in the California history volume, and this story about the Lemurians," Louise reasoned, "I think it's quite likely he started off for the Sierras."

"Maybe we've really picked up a clue!" said Jean, as the girls emerged from the nursing home a few minutes later.

They were so excited about the idea that they failed to notice an elderly patient behind them who was coming outside for his daily stroll. He could not help but overhear Louise say, "There's only one trouble with our theory. If Major Williams didn't have any money, how could he get that far away?"

Suddenly the man behind the sisters touched Louise on the shoulder. "Pardon me," he said. "I heard you talking about Major Williams. He was my best friend here. You say he didn't have any money? He had plenty!"

The Danas looked startled. "He did?" Jean asked. "Where did he get it?"

The elderly man grinned. "I can't tell you that, but this I do know. Major Williams said the money was so well hidden nobody could find it."

Louise and Jean were amazed. If this were true, then Major Williams had plenty of money to take a trip and even, if necessary, to engage a companion! The question was: had he gone far away, or was the girls' hunch right that he had travelled only as far as California gold country?

## CHAPTER III

# Mother Lode Country

EXCITED by their possible clue, Louise and Jean caught a taxi and went to the Crane home.

"You've learned something important, I just know you have. I see it in your eyes!" Janet cried out when she opened the door.

Mrs. Crane rushed forward to hear what the sisters had to tell. Mother and daughter looked astounded as they listened. But when the Danas had finished, Mrs. Crane shook her head.

"You girls have done a wonderful sleuthing job," she complimented them. "I don't want to dampen your spirits, but two things just don't seem to fit in. First, if my father were staying at some motel or private home in northern California where the gold is, I'm sure the police would have found out about it. And the other thing is, where could the Major have hidden any money? I packed his bag when he went to the hospital and later took him a few more clothes while he was at Grandview. He had only a few dollars with him."

Louise was thoughtful for a few seconds, then said, "If Major Williams was telling his friend at the nursing home a secret about his money, there's one place it could have been hidden."

"Where?" Janet and her mother asked.

"Inside his jackets. I mean, either between the lining and the outside or perhaps inside the padding in the shoulders."

Mrs. Crane looked bewildered for a moment, then she smiled at the Danas. "That's a very clever idea. I'm sure we won't find any money hidden in his clothes, but I'll look to be sure. Suppose you all come upstairs with me to my father's room."

When they reached it, Mrs. Crane took out the clothes which she had brought back from the rest home after Major Williams' disappearance.

"One thing I must admit," she said. "For a man, my father was unusually handy with a needle."

She and Janet examined the jackets. The seams above the shoulder padding had been ripped! There was no money hidden inside, but everyone was excited by the discovery.

"The Major removed the money when he planned to leave Grandview!" Janet deduced.

She quickly brought out a suit which had been hanging in the closet for some time. Using a pair of scissors she opened a seam in the shoulder, then ripped open the padding.

Suddenly Mrs. Crane and her daughter gasped. "Money!" Janet cried out. "Oh, Louise, you did guess the Major's secret!"

Neatly tucked inside the padding was money totaling three hundred dollars. Excitedly Mrs. Crane began to examine the other jackets in the closet. Every shoulder pad contained from three hundred to a thousand dollars!

When the job was finished, Mrs. Crane sank into a chair. She buried her face in her hands and sobbed. "My father must have been planning for a long time to leave us!"

Janet rushed to her mother's side. "Oh, please don't cry!" she said. "Grandfather will be found! Now that we know he probably has money with him, he surely isn't suffering from hunger."

Mrs. Crane could not be comforted. She had been under a terrific strain for a long time, and it seemed as if now she could not stand any more. The Danas were greatly embarrassed. Their very helpfulness seemed to have boomeranged!

"We're sorry to have upset you, Mrs. Crane," Louise said kindly. "But don't you think this is really good news?"

Janet's mother looked up. "Oh, I suppose it is. Please forgive me. Dreadful thoughts raced through my head. Since Father wasn't well and strong, I was imagining that he might have been attacked, robbed, and left unconscious some place. He may have had no identification on him and even may have passed away without anyone's being able to notify us."

"You mustn't think that, please!" Jean begged. "Louise and I *promise* to do all we can to search for your father. As soon as we've been to Sacramento to see our Aunt Carol and find out what her mystery is, we'll be in touch with you again."

Mrs. Crane looked at the Danas gratefully. "I don't mean to be unappreciative. I'll take your advice, and try to control my anxiety. When I tell the police about this money, it may give them a new slant to work on in finding the Major."

Louise and Jean bid the Cranes good-by and returned to their hotel. They found Aunt Harriet just saying good-by to someone on the telephone. She told her nieces that she had been talking with the police detective.

"They haven't caught Basil Tripley," she reported. "And they haven't found your ring, Louise. Tripley, they say, is going to be a hard man to trace. His fingerprints are on file, but he's known to be very elusive. No one is registered at any hotel here under that name."

"Of course," Louise put in, "he could be using an alias. Also, Tripley might be miles away from here."

Miss Dana added that Louise's ring had not been found in any of the local pawnshops. "The detective believes that if Tripley is the thief, he still has the sapphire, and is planning to sell it in some other area.

"I gave the detective Aunt Carol's address in Sacramento, so he can reach us there if necessary."

Aunt Harriet now said, "What luck have you had today, girls?"

Quickly Louise and Jean brought her up to date on what they had accomplished. She was astonished to learn of the turn of events.

"I'd say you've been very helpful to the Cranes," she remarked, smiling. "Oh, I do hope Major Williams will be found soon."

"And alive and well," Jean added meaningfully.

The Danas then discussed plans for their trip to Sacramento. Jean phoned and made reservations on a morning plane they could take after breakfast. Later she picked up the tickets. Louise, meanwhile, called Aunt Carol to let her know their time of arrival.

During the evening the girls and Aunt Harriet took a sightseeing tour of San Francisco. The Danas were enthralled by the scenic panoramas, as they travelled up and down the city's steep hills. They especially admired the myriads of lights, including those on the Bay Bridge and the majestic Golden Gate Bridge.

The next morning they were up early and off to the airport. The flight to Sacramento was a short one, but when they reached the Sacramento airport, Louise and Jean noticed that the plane kept circling.

"Traffic must be stacked up," Jean remarked.

Aunt Harriet, seated behind them, stopped the stewardess as she came down the aisle from the pilot's compartment and asked what was causing the delay.

"The pilot has had a little trouble with his landing gear," the young woman replied, "but there's nothing to worry about."

Louise and Jean turned and saw that their aunt was frowning deeply. The sisters knew she was afraid that the plane might run out of fuel and have to make a belly landing.

The "Fasten Seat Belts" sign flashed on.

A moment later the pilot's voice came over the loud-speaker. "I wish to announce that a slight difficulty we had with the landing gear has been eliminated. We shall land in a few minutes."

All the passengers looked relieved. They broke into smiles as the plane's wheels touched the runway and carried them safely to the terminal.

Miss Dana and her nieces alighted and went through the gate. A moment later Jean cried:

"There's Aunt Carol!"

The three visitors hurried toward Mrs. Reed.

As she and the Danas hugged one another, Louise and Jean admired the attractive woman whom they had not seen in many years. She looked much younger than her forty-five years, and was petite and slender, with wavy dark hair.

Aunt Carol was the widow of the brother of the Dana girls' mother. She had a son and a daughter, both of whom were married and living several hundred miles from Sacramento.

After exchanging greetings, Aunt Carol smiled broadly and said, "So, Louise and Jean, you have become detectives!"

"Oh, we're just amateurs, and sometimes miss out completely," Louise quickly assured her.

Miss Harriet Dana made a slight grimace and said, "They don't miss very often, but the two of them scare me to death with some of the dangers they encounter."

As soon as they were in Mrs. Reed's car and driving toward her home, Jean asked, "Aunt Carol, what is the mystery you want us to solve?"

"I can't give you the whole story until we get home," she replied, "because I must show you something in connection with the mystery. This much I can tell you—four generations of Reeds have tried to solve this riddle."

Louise and Jean were startled. Four generations of Reeds had tried and failed! Finally Jean said aloud, "Aunt Carol, are you joking?"

"Indeed I'm not," Mrs. Reed declared. After a pause she added, "I will tell you a little more about the mystery now. Your mother and my deceased husband were the only direct heirs to a buried treasure."

"Wow!" Jean burst out. "Then you and your children and Louise and I would share the treasure!"

"Exactly!" Aunt Carol answered, but would divulge nothing further at the moment.

A little later she pulled into the driveway of a charming Spanish-style house, surrounded by a beautiful garden with a profusion of brilliant flowers.

As soon as they went inside, Aunt Carol showed her guests to attractive bedrooms. The Danas freshened up, and hung a few dresses in the closets. Then, eager to hear more of the story, they joined Aunt Carol in the living room.

"You'll notice that many of our pieces are Oriental," she began. "Most of them are very old, and that has a bearing on the mystery. A direct ancestor of your mother's, Louise and Jean, was a man named Franklin Reed who lived right here in Sacramento.

"He was one of the Forty-niners. That is, he joined the Gold Rush of 1849 to California and came to this area, which is called Mother Lode country. This was the name given to the main

source of the gold here in northern California—
the foothills of the Sierra Nevada mountain range.
Mr. Reed originally came from New England and
brought his wife and only child across the country
in a covered-wagon train from the East."

"How exciting!" Louise exclaimed.

"Exciting, yes," said Aunt Carol. "But they endured severe hardships. Many in the wagon train
died from disease and the harsh weather. Once they
had to go without water for so long that several of
their oxen died. This meant that families had to
double up, causing great inconvenience."

"And there were Indians to battle, I suppose,"
Louise commented.

"Yes, indeed. I imagine Franklin Reed was
thankful when he and his family reached Sacramento alive and unharmed. I understand that they
were not very well when they arrived, and although he still had 'gold fever,' it was some time
before he felt ready to set off and dig."

"Did his wife and son go with him?" Aunt Harriet asked.

"No, they stayed in town. Mr. Reed had opened
a supply store a short time after their arrival and
was doing very well. But in a couple of years he
had a competent clerk who could run the shop
alone.

"The Reeds also had a faithful Chinese servant
named Ying Mee. He was eager to search for gold

too. He went up into Mother Lode country with Franklin. Both of them had some luck. But after a few months Franklin missed his family so much that he gave up his hunt for gold and returned to Sacramento. Ying Mee, however, was really caught by the fever and decided to remain at the diggings. According to reports, he amassed a small fortune and returned to China.

"Nearly six months after this, Franklin received a letter from Ying Mee. It had not been mailed in China, but in San Francisco. Unfortunately, it had been carried by a boat coming to Sacramento and there had been a fire on board. A section of Ying Mee's letter was charred, obliterating the most important part."

"What was that?" Jean asked quickly.

"The location of a chest of gold which Ying Mee had buried for Franklin."

## CHAPTER IV

# Glimpse of a Suspect

"OH!" JEAN and Louise groaned.

"So that's why nobody knows where the treasure is hidden," Jean added. "What does the legible part of Ying Mee's letter say?"

Aunt Carol went to a Chinese cabinet, opened it, and took out a small metal box. Inside lay the old envelope and letter. The note, written on a single sheet of paper, had not been folded. The lower section and the right-hand side of the envelope had been burned away. Aunt Carol handed the letter to the sisters.

"It's in Chinese!" Jean exclaimed in dismay.

Mrs. Reed grinned. She turned back to the cabinet and brought out another piece of paper with a translation. She asked Louise to read it aloud. It said:

*Honorable Mr. Reed:*

*Your humble servant will never forget your many kindnesses. I am returning to my home in Shanghai. Many pardons. To atone for my great discourtesy, I buried an iron chest of nuggets for you. You can identify my unworthy gift by a nugget which I fashioned into the shape of a rocker.*

"A rocker?" Jean interrupted. "Does he mean a rocking chair?"

Aunt Carol laughed. "Up in Mother Lode country a rocker is a device for separating the gold from sand and gravel. Actually it's a wooden trough with a handle. The miners shovelled in what they hoped would be 'pay dirt,' then poured in water. As the rocker was swayed, the sand and dirt were washed away. The pieces of gold fell into a trap made of cleats. The Chinese liked this method and I presume this is why Ying Mee fashioned one of the nuggets into the shape of a rocker."

"It's a fascinating story," Aunt Harriet remarked. "But locating that chest of nuggets sounds more challenging than finding a needle in a haystack."

Aunt Carol turned to her nieces. "Chances of success are slim. That's why my husband never passed the word along to the family. But I thought you young detectives might like to try solving the mystery."

Louise and Jean grinned. "We wouldn't miss it for anything!" Jean said enthusiastically. "But where do we start? What clues do we have to work on?"

"None that I know of," Aunt Carol answered. "Way back in the days when the letter was received, Franklin wrote to Ying Mee at his home in Shanghai. Unfortunately, the letter was returned with a notation that Ying Mee had moved away and his destination was not known."

Miss Dana then told Aunt Carol that the girls had had nothing but excitement ever since they had landed in San Francisco. "They've been asked to solve another mystery, and believe it or not they picked up a clue which might lead to Mother Lode country."

Louise related the story about the missing Major Williams. Suddenly she exclaimed, "Let's combine the two mysteries and look for the buried nuggets while we're trying to locate the Major."

"That's a wonderful idea!" Jean agreed. "And why don't we take Janet along?"

The sisters turned toward their aunts, waiting for comment. The women looked at each other, then Aunt Carol said, "You said 'we.' If you're including me, I'm afraid I can't go along. I have some appointments and work here, so I wouldn't be able to leave for some time, and I know you don't want to wait."

After several seconds of thought, Aunt Harriet asked, "Carol, is it dangerous up in Mother Lode country?"

Mrs. Reed smiled. "If you mean is it civilized, it certainly is. There are traces of the rough, old-time life, but now it's a very modern area. There's only one thing which isn't safe. In the woods and pastures there are many abandoned mine shafts which are still open. The law required people deserting such shafts to cover them properly, but unfortunately too many did not comply."

Miss Dana said she had another reason for asking. "Carol, if Janet Crane can go with Louise and Jean, do you think it would be all right for just the three girls to go up to the Mother Lode country?"

"Oh, yes, perfectly all right. There's a very attractive and well-run motel at the edge of Jackson which I can highly recommend. You can make that your headquarters."

"You mean you don't want to go with us, Aunt Harriet?" Louise asked.

"I'd rather not. Of course if you feel you need a chaperon, telephone me and I'll come right up."

It was decided that Louise would call Janet Crane at once. When Janet heard the story and the proposal, she almost yelled in delight.

"What a wonderful break! Mother is still unconvinced that the Major is up in Mother Lode country, but like you, I have a strong hunch he is.

Will you hold the phone? I'll see if I can get permission to come."

Janet was gone less than a minute and came back, saying she would join the girls the next morning. "I'll take a plane. Will you meet me?"

"Yes!" Louise said. "We'll rent a car for our trip. And, Janet, will you bring a photograph of your grandfather with you? It just occurred to me that if he did come up to this part of California, he probably rented a car here in Sacramento. We'll go around to the different agencies and show them Major Williams' picture."

The following day Aunt Harriet remained at home, but Aunt Carol drove Louise and Jean to meet Janet. Afterward, Mrs. Reed and the three girls visited the various automobile agencies which either rented or sold cars.

At each agency the girls talked to the manager. None of the men recognized Major Williams' picture.

"Well, that hunch of mine brought no results," Louise said to her companions at the last agency. "Anyway, let's rent a car here for ourselves."

This was agreed upon, and in a short while the three girls had picked out a small four-door car. Each showed her driver's license and Louise paid the initial fee. Aunt Carol had parked her car nearby and joined the trio for a "trial run."

"May I drive?" Janet asked.

"Go ahead," Jean replied. She giggled. "We may as well find out right now what kind of chauffeur you are."

Janet climbed in behind the wheel and the four started off. She was just going through the garage exit to the street and saying, "Do I turn left or right?" when suddenly a small dog dashed across the sidewalk directly in front of her.

"Oh!" Janet cried out and jammed on the brakes.

Everyone was thrown off balance, and the little dog howled pitifully.

Janet, although trembling with fright, opened the door and stepped out. The Danas and their aunt also alighted and all rushed toward the little animal. By this time he had started to run, but was still howling as if he were hurt.

"We'd better take him to a veterinarian," Aunt Carol spoke up. "There's one very near here."

Jean sprinted after the small animal who now stopped and looked at her pathetically. "Are you hurt, little fellow?" she said, cautiously extending a hand toward the dog.

He wagged his tail slightly and put out his tongue as if to lick her hand. Sure now that he was not vicious, Jean coaxed him back to the car, and gently placed him inside.

The trip to the animal hospital took only a few minutes. Fortunately, the doctor was in his office and immediately examined the dog.

"This puppy isn't hurt—just mighty scared," he announced. "I'm pretty sure he belongs to a Mrs. Symington. She has brought him here. I'll phone her."

The doctor put in the call and his guess proved to be right. "Mrs. Symington said that she would pick up Trigger here," the veterinarian reported.

Everyone was relieved that Trigger was all right. But Janet still was a bit unnerved by the accident and asked that someone else drive. Louise took the wheel, with Jean seated alongside her. Aunt Carol was dropped off at her car, and the girls drove on.

As they started toward the Reed home, Jean suddenly cried out. She whirled about quickly and stared at a tan convertible going in the opposite direction. It was just turning a corner.

"Louise, quick!" she said. "Go back! Follow that car! I'm sure Basil Tripley was driving it!"

Louise did not hesitate. As soon as it was possible, she made a U-turn and sped after the car which Jean had pointed out.

## CHAPTER V

# The Hint in the Diary

As LOUISE sped down the street after the suspect, she said, "Jean, are you sure the man in the car was Basil Tripley?"

"How could I forget that face!" Jean replied wryly.

By this time Louise had reached the corner. The light turned red and she was forced to stop. The other car was no longer in sight. Nevertheless, when the light turned green, Louise rounded the corner. As she drove along, Jean and Janet scanned the road and the cross streets for a tan convertible. It was nowhere to be seen.

"What a shame I couldn't get his license number," Jean said in disappointment. "But as soon as we get back to Aunt Carol's, let's call hotels and motels to see if Tripley's registered at any of them." Ten minutes later she began her quest of the suspected thief, but had no luck.

Just then Aunt Carol, who had stopped to do some shopping, came into the house. Quickly the girls told of their recent experience.

"Basil Tripley," Jean told her aunt, "is the kind of man who gives you the shivers. His eyes are a faded blue and rather prominent. He wears his blond hair very long, and he's skinny. But the main thing is the obnoxious way he talks and acts."

"He sounds like a dreadful person," Mrs. Reed remarked.

"We'd better notify the police," Louise said, adding with determination, "If there's any chance of finding the thief who took my ring, I want to do it as soon as possible."

She called, and the officer on duty thanked her for the clue. Louise gave him Mrs. Reed's name and address and he promised to get in touch with the house should he have any success in locating the suspect.

"We'd better have some lunch," Aunt Carol said. "Do you girls want to help?"

Aunt Harriet looked at the others, a twinkle in her eye. "All you have to do is sit down at the table," she said. "My hands weren't idle while you were away."

Miss Dana had prepared a delicious luncheon—cream of celery soup, chicken salad with sliced tomatoes, and custard pudding topped with currant jelly.

Aunt Carol was delighted. "I'm afraid I can't add anything to this meal but homemade biscuits." She produced some chocolate-, vanilla-, and coco-nut-flavoured squares.

When they had finished eating, the girls washed the dishes. Then Louise and Jean asked Aunt Carol if she had any family records which would help them in solving the mystery of the buried nuggets.

"For instance, old letters, a diary, or any nota-tions that would give us an idea of the character and traits of Ying Mee," Louise suggested.

Mrs. Reed said she had several boxes of letters which Franklin Reed had written to his wife while he was digging for gold. She brought them for the girls to read. There was complete silence for a long time as each made notes. Finally they were ready to compare their findings.

"I'm afraid I didn't come up with very much," Jean spoke up. "Ying Mee was a very patient, hon-est, and lovable person. He did not mind hardships, and it was amazing, when food was scarce, how he could live on rice day after day!"

"Can't you just see him?" Janet said. "Here it says he walked with short, quick steps, often mut-tering in a singsong tone. When Mr. Reed asked him what he was saying, Ying Mee explained that he was counting. He was excellent in mathematics, and a whiz with the abacus counter."

"I notice," said Aunt Carol, "that Ying Mee

also refers to an abacus by its Chinese name—
*suan-pan*."

Louise then read from her notes. "Ying Mee
loved nature, especially big trees. He would stand
and gaze at one for long periods and try to make a
sketch of it." After a pause she added, "This might
be a possible clue to a hiding place for the nuggets
—some beautiful big tree."

"Which by this time probably has been cut
down," Jean said practically.

Janet remarked that after Franklin Reed had left,
Ying Mee probably had spent his leisure time with
Chinese in the mining camps. "I understand that
there were many, many of them hunting gold in
those communities. They had their own joss
houses—temples, that is—and restaurants."

From the old letters, they learned that Franklin
Reed had dug gold at Jackson, Volcano, Sutter
Creek, and Amador City.

"So it's likely Ying Mee didn't go anywhere
else," Louise remarked. "Anyway, let's confine
our search to those places."

Aunt Harriet smiled. "You can't dig up all of
Amador County," she said. "And you won't be
able to work on private property, either. I'd say
your search will be rather limited."

Louise and Jean agreed. Then suddenly Louise
caught a look of sadness in Janet's eyes. Instantly
she realized that it must seem to the girl as though

the sisters were more interested in finding the family treasure than in helping her locate the missing Major Williams.

Louise left her chair and went over to sit beside Janet on a couch. "I'd say that the main thing we're going to do in Amador County is hunt for your grandfather," she said kindly. "Of course we'd like to locate those nuggets, but we're certainly going to make every effort to solve your mystery."

Janet brightened, her gratefulness apparent. "Oh, thank you for saying that."

"I suppose you'll start early tomorrow morning?" Aunt Carol asked.

"Right after breakfast," Jean replied.

That evening the three girls packed jeans, shirts, sweaters, and sturdy shoes. Everyone was up early the following day and by eight o'clock the girls were ready to leave, and after exchanging fond good-bys with Aunt Carol and Aunt Harriet, drove off.

"Please be careful!" Miss Dana called after them.

As they went through the city, Janet pointed out various sights of interest. The Danas were high in their praise of the stately capitol building with its impressive dome, and adjacent park with palm trees and flowering camellia bushes.

"I'm glad they picked Sacramento to be the capital of California," Janet said. "As you see, this area along the Sacramento River is semitropical. It's a wonderful place to live. I used to visit here frequently."

"Didn't I read somewhere," Louise asked, "that Sacramento is called the city of camellias?"

Janet nodded. "Aren't they exquisite?"

Louise, who was driving, followed Route 16 for an hour and a half. For late autumn, it was an unusually warm, dry day. They passed mile after mile of grassy fields, turned to yellows and warm browns. The expanse was dotted with honey-coloured foliage and an occasional group of Digger pines, their drooping. scraggly branches laden with large, dark cones.

Finally Louise reached the famous Highway 49, appropriately named after the old miners. She turned right and in a short time came to the old village of Drytown. The girls stopped for lemon sodas at a roadside store and were told by the young man in charge that this was the oldest town in Mother Lode country.

"At one time the population here was eight thousand white people, mostly Mexicans, and two thousand Chinese. Among the American families were the Boones. Molly Boone, a direct descendant of Daniel Boone, was born here in 1849."

"How interesting!" said Louise. "Was much gold mined here?"

"Oh, plenty! Why, it's said even the roots of

the tussocks of grass along the creeks and gulches contained four to five dollars in gold." The clerk grinned. "There's still gold around here if you want to try your hand at using a pan."

"That sounds exciting," Jean spoke up. "I think before I leave Amador County, I'll do just that."

The next town on the girls' route was Amador City, which lay between two hills. As they rounded a sharp curve in the centre and turned right up the slope which led out of town, Jean called out:

"Oh, look! Louise, do stop!"

Her sister pulled over and parked. On the girls' left, situated atop an embankment, was one of the most fascinating buildings they had ever seen. High across the front walls, above a long porch, there was a sign:

## GOLD RUSH
### Trading Post & Museum

The porch was filled with carved wooden figures and antiques from the days of the Forty-niners. The life-size figure of a Chinese seated at a rocker caught their attention. Near him stood a woman, dressed in a frilly white blouse, long black skirt, and fancily trimmed sailor hat. Farther along were various gadgets used by the miners.

"Let's go and see what's inside the museum," Janet suggested. "Maybe the owner can give me some clues to the Major."

The girls parked the car, then went up the steps at the side of the porch. When Jean opened the door a bell sounded, and a stocky man, wearing a gray goatee, western hat and cowboy boots, came from a back room. He introduced himself as Frank Fish, and said he was the owner of the place. The girls told him they would like to make a tour of the museum.

"Certainly. Go right ahead."

The visitors paid the fee and went through a small gate into the main part of the exhibit. All were astounded to see the large collection of artifacts and finely made antiques which filled the walls, showcases, and part of the floor. Just then a record which Mr. Fish had made describing the various articles began to play. Everything was identified by number and the girls kept exclaiming in awe at the pictures, weapons, jewellery, costumes, and many Oriental pieces.

"This collection must be worth a great deal of money!" Janet remarked.

"It is," Mr. Fish replied, smiling, "and I dug up most of it myself. I'm a treasure hunter."

"How exciting!" Jean exclaimed.

When the girls finished the tour, they found Mr. Fish standing behind a glass-enclosed counter.

In it were pieces of jewellery made of nuggets. Janet decided to buy one for her mother and the Danas bought two, one for Aunt Harriet, the other for Aunt Carol. As Louise and Jean gazed at the nugget jewellery, they wondered if they would be successful in their own quest for nuggets secreted by Ying Mee.

"Mr. Fish," Janet spoke up, "have you, by any chance, met an elderly man around here by the name of Williams?" She brought out the photograph. "He's Major Williams, retired."

Mr. Fish shook his head. "No, I haven't seen this man. Are you looking for him?"

Janet told the story of her missing grandfather and asked Mr. Fish, "If you should by chance meet Major Williams, please have him get in touch with me at our motel in Jackson."

"I'll be very happy to," he said.

In further conversation, the girls learned that Mr. Fish had several hobbies, one of them being the carving of wooden Indians. "Would you like to see my workshop?" he asked them.

"Oh, yes," the three girls chorused.

Mr. Fish led the way from the museum out to the porch and into an adjoining building. Once more the girls were startled at what they saw. In one corner stood a taller than life-size Indian, which Mr. Fish said weighed four hundred pounds.

"How realistic he looks!" Louise remarked.

Mr. Fish smiled. "Geronimo will look even more so after I get him stained and put on his war paint."

On a long workbench lay a half-finished statue of another Indian. As Jean lingered to admire the finished figure, the other girls moved over to watch Mr. Fish give a wood-carving demonstration with a chisel.

As they watched, there was a tremendous roar and whistling sound overhead which the girls recognized as those of a jet plane. Within seconds, the whole building shook from the vibration.

Just then Jean looked toward the others, and giggled. "Goodness! Feels almost like an earthquake!"

But at the same moment Louise saw with horror that the Indian figure in the corner was swaying. Any moment it would topple on Jean!

Louise screamed, "Jean! Look out!" and jumped forward to drag her sister out of danger.

The treasure hunter was even quicker. With a leap he reached the Indian and pushed it back into place!

The danger over, Jean breathed a sigh of relief and thanked Mr. Fish profusely. He grinned. "I guess Geronimo doesn't like modern jets."

Jean smiled wryly. "And he was going to take it out on me!"

As the girls followed the museum owner outside, Louise noticed an instrument standing on the porch which she had not seen before. The bottom of the device was a flat metal piece about a foot square. There was a long, slanted handle to which was attached a metal headpiece with earphones. "What is this?" she asked.

"A metal detector," Mr. Fish answered. "When I have time, I go around Mother Lode country treasure hunting. You know, lots of the old miners buried their treasures and much of the gold has never been dug up."

The three girls looked at one another, then Louise asked, "Mr. Fish, did you ever come across a chest of nuggets and find one among them beaten into an unusual design?"

## CHAPTER VI

# Tailing Wheels

THE proprietor of the Gold Rush Museum looked at the Danas and Janet quizzically. "No, I never found any unusually designed nuggets. Are you looking for some?"

Before any of the girls could answer, Mr. Fish heard a car stop in front of the museum. At once he went to the end of the porch and called back over his shoulder, "I'll have to say good-by now. More sightseers. But come back again sometime, won't you?"

The girls thanked him for showing them his workshop and then said good-by. They drove up the hill and on to the next town, which was Sutter Creek. It had a thriving main street, with old and new buildings side by side.

"You probably know this town was named after the man who started the Gold Rush," said

Janet. "He owned a whipsaw mill at Coloma, about thirty miles from here, with a partner named Marshall. One morning Mr. Marshall went down to the stream to look things over and discovered small pieces of gold."

"Then word spread like wildfire, I suppose," Jean remarked.

"Yes. The Gold Rush lasted for a good many years. First the miners just used pans to wash their diggings. Then came the rocker, sometimes called a cradle. And still later, hydraulic mining where great streams of water were played on the earth and gravel from giant hoses. Finally modern deep mining began, with shafts down into the earth and tunnels running from them in various directions, depending on where there was a vein of gold."

Jean chuckled. "Janet, you really know your California, don't you?"

Janet looked off into the distance. "I didn't see much of my grandfather when I was a little girl, but whenever I did he would tell me stories of the early days of our state. And he often talked about this very area. I never dreamed that he'd—well, come to this place as a refuge." She smiled at her friends. "I guess it takes a detective's mind to put two and two together. Oh, girls, I'm *so* hopeful now of finding the Major somewhere up here."

When they reached the outskirts of Jackson,

the girls spotted the motel which Mrs. Reed had
suggested. It was a long, Spanish-type building,
erected on two levels of ground. The lower part
had bedrooms facing a parking area and a lovely
garden and swimming pool. The pleasant woman
proprietor showed the Dana girls to one room, and
Janet to another directly next door.

As soon as they had unpacked, the girls set off
for town about a mile distant. On the way, high
on a hill beyond the road, they saw the tall, der-
ricklike wooden structure which Janet said was
called a headframe. It covered a deep, vertical
mine shaft. Clustered about it were abandoned,
weather-beaten buildings.

"Like so many mines in Mother Lode country,
this one is not being worked any more," Janet told
the Danas. "But it's rumoured that any day they
may start up again."

The town of Jackson was a modern, thriving
one. Many of the old buildings were still standing,
notably the attractive hotel at the end of the main
street. But new fronts had been put on many first-
floor shops and one had to gaze upward to see the
old-style railing and windows which indicated
that this county seat of Amador had been as large
and even more bustling from the 1850's through
1942.

Louise parked the car, then the girls started making inquiries, first at the hotel, then the shops. In

every case they showed Major Williams' picture and asked if anyone had seen him. No one had.

While in a gift-toy-stationery shop, one of the women clerks became curious about the girls' reason for being in Jackson. They told Janet's story, but kept Ying Mee's treasure a secret.

"Well, I hope you find him," the woman said. "Poor old man!" She leaned across the counter. "You all sound as though you're very interested in the history of this place. I have a copy of an old diary written by a Forty-niner. It was in an antique bureau I bought at an auction. I'll sell the diary cheap."

Jean was on the verge of saying no, when Louise asked, "How much do you want for it?"

"Only five dollars, and it's worth a lot more."

"Do you have the diary here?" Louise inquired.

"Yes." The woman reached under the counter and took out a very large handbag. She opened it and produced a sheaf of papers clipped together.

Louise took it and quickly read half the first page. Then she glanced at a few more pages, and to her friends' amazement, said quickly, "I'll buy this."

When the three girls reached the street, Jean demanded, "How do you know that's genuine, Sis? It may be a fake."

Louise smiled widely. "Maybe. But, believe it or not, I saw the name Ying Mee in this diary!"

At once all the girls wanted to read the diary sheets, so they walked directly back to the car. Settling themselves on the back seat, they quickly started looking through the entries. In the early part the diarist, named Michael Sanderson, told of his overland trip in a covered wagon and the many hardships he had endured. The second part of the diary described his life as a prospector and told of various diggings.

"Here's the part about Ying Mee," said Louise.

Excitedly the girls read it. Mr. Sanderson had been attacked by a thief who had started to run off with the miner's bag of nuggets. Ying Mee had arrived just in time to rescue the bag of gold and capture the thief. Jean read aloud:

" 'The Chinese saved my life. He is a good fellow. I guess he has dug a lot of gold himself. He is going back to his native land soon.' "

"This certainly sounds as if he was the same Ying Mee who worked for your ancestor," Janet remarked. "Where did the holdup take place?"

Louise turned back several pages until she came to a notation that said Mr. Sanderson was about to begin work in Volcano. She learned that it was here that the attempted robbery had occurred.

"Then Ying Mee may have buried our treasure in Volcano!" Jean exclaimed. With a sigh she added, "But where?"

As Louise read on a little farther, she said, "Perhaps Ying Mee hid the nuggets somewhere else. It says here he left for Jackson."

Louise and Jean looked so glum over the tremendous task ahead of them that Janet tried to cheer them.

"Jackson was always an important place in Mother Lode country," she told her friends. "The date when Ying Mee was in Jackson, and the approximate time we figure from the letter he wrote to Franklin Reed, coincide pretty well. Why don't you girls do some digging right here?"

"First I think we should drive around and get to know this place better," Louise suggested. "Then we can decide where to start our work."

The girls consulted a helpful pamphlet they had obtained from the Amador County Chamber of Commerce office in Jackson. They decided that their first trip out of town would be to Jackson Gate a mile and a half away. On the way, Janet read from the pamphlet.

" 'Here stand two gigantic wheels built in 1902, part of a great system for carrying the mill waste from the Kennedy Mine. A series of wooden gravity flumes and wheels at various levels carried the waste, called tailings, to a high ridge where it was dumped.

" 'The tailing wheels were equipped with one hundred and seventy-six buckets, a belt drive, and an electric motor,' " Janet read on.

"I see the wheels!" Jean cried, and pointed to a hillside on their left. "Wow, they really are big!"

Louise parked and the girls went through the little gate into pasture land below them.

"This whole area has been deeded to Amador County," Janet remarked.

When they reached the top of the hill, the girls gazed in awe at the largest of the tailing wheels.

"This pamphlet says," Janet went on, "the wheel is sixty-eight feet in diameter and raised the tailings straight up a distance of forty-eight feet."

"The buckets have been removed," Jean observed.

Suddenly Janet whistled. "Do you know how much gold was taken out of the Kennedy Mine?" she asked. "Forty-five million dollars!"

"Amazing!" Louise murmured.

The three friends picked their way along the slope which was thick with manzanita shrubs, some of their crooked limbs holding clusters of little red "apples." Gay toyon berrybushes grew along the path, which led to a winding boulder-filled stream flanked by low-growing alder trees.

"Do you suppose Ying Mee hid the chest of nuggets along this stream?" Jean asked excitedly.

Louise shrugged. "It's as good a place as any for us to start digging," she said. "Let's go back to town and buy equipment for gold panning, anyway. I'd like to pick up a nugget or two."

Janet begged to be excused from the trip. "I'd like to do a little more sleuthing around town myself. And I'll do something to help you. I'll go to the museum and look through old records and pictures to see if I can get any clues to Ying Mee."

"That *would* be a great help," Louise said.

The girls ate a late lunch in a restaurant in town, then separated. The Danas went to a hardware store and asked for the necessary equipment to hunt for nuggets on or near the surface. The young male clerk was extremely interested in assisting them.

"I've done a little placer mining myself," he said, smiling. "It sure is a big thrill to find something."

He showed them the special type of pan used for washing gold. It was round, fairly large, and had sloping sides.

The rest of the equipment included a large spoon, an old file bent on the narrow end, a pair of tweezers, a small magnet, a shovel, a miner's pick, and a tiny clear glass bottle with a tight screw top.

"I hope you'll fill this bottle with nuggets," the clerk said with a grin. As he gave Louise change, he added, "Best of luck. Let me know how you get on."

"We will!"

Louise and Jean set off in high hope. A short time

later they were back at the stream below the great tailing wheels, with their equipment lined up around them.

"Let's just shovel a little pay dirt into the pan right from the stream," Jean suggested impatiently.

She dropped several shovelfuls of sand into the pan, then sat down on a rock and filled the pan three-quarters full of water. As she swirled it around, the sand and gravel gradually floated away. Soon Jean was down to the last washing.

Her eyes were glued intently on the contents. Was she imagining it or did she see some flecks of gold?

Louise had been watching the operation closely, but suddenly she heard a noise among the bushes above the girls. Turning quickly, she saw an old man with white hair and a flowing white beard peering at the girls. He was dressed like an old-time miner, including a large-brimmed hat.

"He looks like something out of a picture!" Louise thought, and waited for the man to come forward.

But instead, the instant he realized that Louise had seen him, the stranger turned and vanished!

# CHAPTER VII

# Gold Fever

"JEAN!" Louise exclaimed. "Did you see that white-haired man among the bushes?"

"No."

Quickly Louise described him. "He certainly looked like an old-timer. He might be able to give us some help in locating Major Williams or even Ying Mee's buried treasure."

Jean hardly heard what her sister said. She exclaimed, "Look here! Gold!"

Louise peered into the pan. Three very tiny nuggets lay in the indentations at the bottom. "How wonderful!" she exclaimed. "But, Jean, I think we should try to talk to that old man I saw."

She dashed off, crying, "Stop! Please stop, sir! I must talk to you!"

There was no answer. Was the old man hard of

hearing or was he deliberately avoiding her? Surely he could not have retreated so far that he could not hear her voice.

Jean, not wishing to leave the panning equipment and unable to gather it all together quickly enough to follow her sister, remained where she was. After several minutes had gone by, Jean became anxious about Louise. She recalled Aunt Carol's warning of the uncovered mine shafts into which one might inadvertently fall.

"Gold or no gold, I'm going after Louise," Jean determined. She left everything lying on the ground and hurried after her sister, calling her name. Presently Louise's answer came.

Jean, vastly relieved, caught up to her. "What happened?"

"I've looked in every direction," Louise reported, "but the white-haired man seems to have vanished."

"Maybe he's hiding in some old cave or mine tunnel," Jean suggested.

The two girls searched the area for some time, then gave up.

"I'm sure we can find out in town who that man is," Louise stated. "There can't be very many people around here who look like him."

She and Jean returned to their gold panning. Louise unscrewed the round glass bottle and held it over the pan. Carefully Jean picked up the tiny gold nuggets with the tweezers and dropped them into the bottle. Louise screwed the top back on.

Jean laughed. "Even if we don't find Ying Mee's chest of nuggets, we've made a start toward another family fortune!"

Louise chuckled and picked up the pan. "Suppose you shovel in some sand and gravel this time, Sis, and I'll see if my luck's as good as yours."

Jean took the shovel and went to work. When the pan was two-thirds full, she stopped and Louise began the washing operation. She set the pan on the bottom of the shallow stream, holding it steady with her left hand. With her right she stirred up the mass and broke the lumps of dirt with her fingers.

"My goodness! You're scientific about this," Jean remarked.

Louise smiled. "That diary told exactly how the Forty-niners used to pan gold, so I thought I'd do it right."

She now grasped both sides of the pan firmly, tipped it at a slight angle toward her, and gently shook it to and fro.

As the sand and gravel began to ooze from the pan, Louise said with a grin, "This is called sloughing off."

"Go ahead, professor. Tell me the rest," Jean teased.

"All right, you asked for it," said Louise. "The reason the gold particles go to the bottom and the other substances wash away is because gold is over seven times heavier. It has an atomic weight of 197.2, which is very heavy."

Finally there was nothing left in the pan but black sand. Louise took the pan from the water, drained it, then picked up the magnet. One by one she took out the grains of sand. Underneath were revealed tiny nuggets of gleaming gold!

"I've never been more excited in my life!" she exclaimed happily.

The girls worked until late in the afternoon. They had many failures, but were rewarded by filling up half the tiny bottle with nuggets of various shapes and sizes.

During the whole period they had kept looking among the bushes to see if the white-whiskered man had returned to watch them. But so far as they knew, he had not.

Finally the girls gathered up their equipment and started back. "I'm afraid I have gold fever!" Louise said as the girls climbed the hill.

"That makes two of us!" Jean agreed.

They passed the great tailing wheels and went down the other side to where they had left their car. When they arrived at the motel, they found Janet very despondent. Although she had spent hours conversing with various people in town, she

had not received any lead to Major Williams'
whereabouts.

Jean gave her a quick hug. "You mustn't be
discouraged. A sleuth, as we've found out, has
many setbacks. Tell you what. Tomorrow we'll
just search for your grandfather."

Janet brightened. "Oh, you're wonderful," she
said. "I guess part of the reason I felt bad was because I found nothing to help you, either. I
looked through old records and pictures at the
museum and at the newspaper offices, but didn't
come across anything about Ying Mee."

Louise, who had sat down on the edge of Janet's
bed, remarked, "I've read that when people for
one reason or another tire of the life they're living,
and go off into the wilderness or on some kind of
an adventure, they may take up some hobby they
had in their childhood. Can you think of anything
in particular the Major liked to do as a boy?"

Janet thought for some time. Finally she said,
"The only thing I can recall is that the Major
owned a very fine harmonica—one of the two-
octave, diatonic type. My mother told me that
when she was a little girl her father played it often
and she thought he was marvellous."

"Didn't he continue to play as he got older?"
Louise asked.

"I never heard him. In fact, I understand that he
lost the harmonica and never bought another."

"It's a mighty slim clue," Louise admitted. "But Jean and I try to make it a rule never to overlook anything which may help solve a mystery."

True to their promise, the Danas told Janet the following morning that they were ready to start a new hunt for Major Williams. Since no one in town seemed to have noticed him, Louise suggested that they do a little investigating in the area where she had glimpsed the old man with the white beard.

"If your grandfather," she said to Janet, "was trying to find the cave where the ancient Lemurians secreted gold, he surely would have tramped through the woods. Perhaps the old-timer met him."

"That's a good idea," Janet agreed. "Let's start right now looking for him!"

But though the girls searched all morning they found no trace of the elderly stranger.

At last Jean announced she was starving. "I suggest we go back to Jackson and have lunch."

When the Danas and Janet were seated in a restaurant across the street from a variety store, Louise said, "As soon as we finish eating, let's go over to that shop and find out if they sell harmonicas."

Janet leaned across the table. "Do you think the Major wanted to start playing again and went there to buy one?"

"It's a slight chance," said Louise, "but we don't want to leave any clue unturned! We can also ask about the elderly man with the long white beard."

When the three girls entered the shop they found a counter where harmonicas were sold. A youth of seventeen, very thin and pale, with blond hair straggling in thick wisps over his forehead, stood there. He eyed the girls in a rather insolent manner. Then he picked up a harmonica and began to examine it.

Louise spoke to the young woman clerk behind the counter. "Can you tell me anything about an old man who has a long beard? My sister and I saw him out by the tailing wheels."

When the clerk shook her head, Louise tried another tack. Pointing to the harmonicas, she asked, "Have you recently sold one of these to a man with white hair? He's—"

Before she could continue, the scraggly-haired young man gave a raucous laugh. Then, imitating the voice of a very old person, he said squeakily, "Oh, sure. Grandpa's a ripsnorter. Haven't yuh heard? We took him into our high school band!"

Several customers around burst into laughter. Encouraged by this approval of his funmaking, the youth went on, "I'll show yuh how to play this here thing." He moved the harmonica back and forth between his lips, playing discordant notes and an uncertain melody.

Janet and the Danas were completely disgusted. All three felt like telling the youth that poking fun at elderly people was a poor pastime. Instead, they ignored him completely.

Louise once more turned to the clerk.

"We're very eager to obtain some information about a man named Major Williams," she said. "A harmonica may be a clue. Can you help us?"

## CHAPTER VIII

# The Harmonica Player

"So you can't take a joke, eh?" the unpleasant high school youth said scornfully to the Danas and their companion. He laid down the harmonica and moved off.

The woman clerk winked at Louise and said, "You mustn't mind Hep Delaney. He doesn't mean anything by his crazy jokes. He's kind of a goofy kid but he plays the harmonica pretty well."

"He's certainly rude," Janet remarked.

Louise described the tall, slender, smooth-shaven man with white hair and asked if anyone resembling him had bought a harmonica there recently.

The clerk shook her head. "Nobody like that. My only customers have been kids. You folks aren't from town, are you?"

"No, we're not," Jean said. "We live a long way from here, as a matter of fact. But we're trying to clear up a mystery." She introduced herself, Louise, and Janet, and mentioned where they were staying.

"This Major Williams—does he play the harmonica?" the clerk asked, interested.

"He used to many years ago," Janet replied.

As she said this a good-looking man of about twenty-five walked toward the girls. He was the outdoor type, ruddy and muscular.

"Hello, Dusty," the clerk said to him. "What can I do for you?"

"Well nothing, Sue," he answered. "I overheard these girls talking about a harmonica player and I thought I'd tell them something I came across a little while ago."

Sue introduced the man as Dusty Hooper, a truck driver for a rock-and-gravel company. Dusty was his nickname.

"I've just made a run from Volcano over here," he said. "About halfway along I stopped in the shade to eat my lunch. Next thing I knew I heard harmonica music in the distance. Boy, was that ever nifty playing!"

"Oh!" cried Janet.

Could the player have been the missing Major? the girls wondered.

"Wh-where was the person playing the harmonica?" Janet asked tensely.

"Sorry, but I don't know," Dusty replied. "I

didn't see the player. The music might have come from a cabin, from the woods, or even from somewhere farther along the road."

Janet was quivering with excitement. "Louise and Jean," she said, "let's go there right now and see if we can find the harmonica player."

Dusty Hooper gave the girls directions to the location, which he said they could find easily. The area was thick with ponderosa pine, some oaks, and many bushes.

"The land on the left of the road goes downhill slightly, but on your right there's a sharp rise. At the exact spot where I stopped there's a canyon, with a wide stream coming down through it. The place is sure pretty. You can't miss it."

The girls thanked him, and Dusty wished them luck in their quest. Jean took the wheel of their car, and soon was driving along the scenic, mountainous road. Green and yellow predominated in the trees and shrubs. The day was warm for November and the air clear and invigorating.

When they reached the mountain stream which carved a narrow, shallow canyon, the girls debated whether they should start their search to the left or to the right.

"I think Janet should decide," Louise spoke up.

"Okay. Left."

Jean parked the car far over on the road. Quickly the three girls made their way among the bushes and trees, watching carefully for snakes and uncovered mine shafts, as well as any sign of a cabin or person in the woods. They walked for nearly an hour without seeing anything of particular interest so far as the mystery was concerned. Finally the weary searchers sat down on a boulder to rest.

"I'm beginning to feel like one of those pioneer women," Jean said with a tired chuckle.

"That gives me an idea," said Louise. "Suppose I read you a bedtime story."

The other two girls laughed, wondering what Louise meant. From a pocket in her jeans she pulled out the first few pages of the copy of the prospector's diary which she had purchased.

"I want to read the whole thing thoroughly," she said. "Suppose I start now."

"Oh, don't read the part about the beginning of the wagon train," Jean begged. "Just California."

Louise picked out a section marked June 3, 1849. The diarist narrated that the night before there had been great excitement in their encampment in Nevada. Since Indians had been molesting them, it was decided when making camp for the next night they would protect their horses as well as themselves from attack.

" 'We built a square enclosure of our waggons,' " Louise read, smiling at the quaint misspelling, of which there were several. " 'The horses were put inside the enclosure. But we forgot about our cows. During the night the Indians slipped up and took six of them away. This morning we thought they were gone for good.

" 'But one of the families was missing a cow named Bossy that had a bell on her neck. Several of us men volunteered to go out and try to find the cows. We did. Bossy gave away their position. The Indians had not had time yet to slaughter any of the cows. When the Indians saw us coming with rifles, they ran, so we got all the cows back. You cannot get ahead of Unkle Sam's men!' "

The girls laughed. Louise continued. Soon she came to a notation for June 8. "Listen to this:

" 'Today our meat supply was very low. We met some friendly Indians. When they heard about our misfortune they gave us some dead prairie dogs and screech owls. I could not stummick any of it, but the Indians think they are tasty!' "

"Ugh!" said Janet. "I'll stick to roast beef!"

"And me to chicken," Jean added. "Or even a peanut-butter sandwich!"

Louise folded the diary sheets and put them back into her pocket. "End of story for today." She stood up. "Let's go! I vote we search now on the opposite side of the road."

The others voiced agreement. They trekked back to the road, crossed it, and started up the hillside along the rushing mountain stream.

Suddenly Jean, who was in the lead, stopped.

"I hear something moving—above us," she whispered. "I don't know whether it's an animal or a human being."

The girls stood still and listened. Finally Jean called out boldly, "Who's there?"

No answer came. Then Janet yelled loudly, "Major! Major Williams! Are you here?"

Still no response.

"It must have been an animal," Louise said philosophically. "And fortunately there aren't any dangerous ones here."

At that moment they were startled by hearing what sounded like the cracking of a tree limb. The next moment the limb sailed through the air directly toward them. Quick as lightning the three jumped out of its path, and the limb went by them. It crashed and splintered against a pine tree farther below.

"Do you suppose someone threw that?" Jean asked suspiciously.

The girls gazed upward intently, their eyes roaming the forest. They could see no one and now everything was quiet.

Louise happened to be standing alongside a large rock. Without realizing it, she had put her hand down directly over a crevice in the stone. The next moment something squirmed under her hand!

## CHAPTER IX

# Landslide

LOUISE cried out in alarm and pulled away her hand. At the same instant, a three-foot-long snake slithered from the crevice in the rock! The reptile was black with a white stripe running down its back.

"Look out!" Janet cried out. "That's a California king snake—a constrictor!"

The snake apparently had no intention of staying, for he slithered away quickly through the undergrowth.

Jean grinned. "Sis," she teased, "I'm glad he didn't coil around your neck and give you a squeeze."

"Yes," said Janet, "we might have been missing a good detective."

Louise smiled gamely, but was a bit shaken. "We'd better watch our step more carefully when we go through the woods!"

Janet explained that California was fortunate in having few poisonous snakes. "There are rattle-snakes, though, in the hills here. Usually all snakes are hibernating at this time of year, but it's been such a warm fall many of them may still be above-ground."

Louise grimaced. "I'm lucky the snake I touched wasn't a rattler."

In the excitement the three friends had forgotten they were trying to find whoever might have thrown the tree limb at them. They now clambered up the steep ascent to try to find the culprit. Some thirty feet above, Jean exclaimed:

"Someone *was* here! He probably *did* toss that limb!" She pointed to a series of footprints in the ground. "Let's follow them!"

The girls set off. At times the prints disappeared completely, but the girls were able to pick them up again. The tracks ran parallel to the road, then turned downward, ending at the road.

"Here's where our mysterious stranger evaporated," Jean said in disgust. "Did he walk away on the hard surface? Or was he in a car? There are several tire marks here."

Louise crossed the road and examined the ground for footprints, in case the man was eluding them in that part of the woods. She saw none.

Jean went back to examine the prints. Suddenly a puzzled frown came over her face.

"What's the matter?" Janet asked her.

Jean said she was sure that the set of footprints which came downhill were not the same as those running parallel on the slope. "I'm going back up there and look," she said.

The others waited while Jean climbed the hillside. Presently she called to Louise and Janet to join her. When they reached her side, she was standing on a large flat rock.

"I was right. Look over here. The first footprints we were following continue right on through the woods. The person who made them must have crossed over this boulder. We were sidetracked by following a different set down the hill. The second ones come from up above." She pointed and the others could see them plainly.

Janet shook her head. "You're amazing, Jean."

Her friend chuckled. "Janet," she asked, "did your grandfather walk with his feet pointed absolutely straight ahead?"

"Why, yes."

"Then one thing is settled," said Jean. "These footprints that parallel the rock do not belong to the Major. If you'll look carefully, you'll see that the left foot turns out slightly." She grinned. "I'd say the mysterious stranger should take a trip to a shoemaker. His right heel is badly run over."

Janet shook her head in utter astonishment at the deduction. Then she made an observation of her own. "These other footprints we followed down the hill don't belong to the Major, either. They're much too short."

Jean grinned. "Congratulations, Janet. You'll be a detective yet!"

Louise had been thoughtful during the discussion. Now she spoke up. "Shall we keep trying to find the person who may have thrown that tree limb?"

Janet shook her head. "I'm getting dreadfully tired," she admitted. "Since none of these footprints belong to the Major, I think we'd better give up for now on this hunt. Do you realize we came out here to find a harmonica player, and we haven't heard a single note—or even seen a cabin where the player might live?"

"You're right," Louise agreed. "Let's go back to the motel and have a swim."

"I vote for that," Jean put in.

The girls decided to take a zigzag course on the way to their car. Perhaps they *would* see a cabin!

In a short time they came to a huge mound of earth rising some thirty feet into the air. It was covered with brown weeds, grass, and a few squatty bushes. Automatically the girls walked around the foot of it.

"I imagine that enormous heap was tailings from some diggings around here. We'd better watch our step for an open mine shaft," Janet warned.

The girls picked their way along carefully. They saw no open or depressed spots in the ground, but in a few minutes discovered the entrance to a limestone cave under the mound. They stopped and gazed inside the opening. It was dark within, and they could see little.

Jean grabbed Louise's arm. "What a wonderful hiding place for a treasure!" she said. "Maybe this is where Ying Mee left the nuggets!"

"That's right," Louise replied. "I suppose we should investigate, but we didn't bring our flashlights."

"Let's come back first thing tomorrow morning," Jean proposed.

Janet, meanwhile, had been peering with rapt attention toward the cave's interior. "If the Major is trying to hide," she remarked, "this would be an ideal place." A look of sadness came over her face. "Also, if he were ill he—he might have gone into a place like this, and—and—"

Their friend could not finish, and the Danas realized what she was thinking—that her beloved grandfather *might* be inside the darkened cavern but no longer living.

She begged the girls to investigate the cave as far as the light would permit.

"All right," Louise agreed. "But remember, we may have an enemy nearby. Someone should stand guard, while two of us go in."

Jean and Janet thought this sensible. Louise offered to stay outside and keep her eyes open for intruders. At once Janet and Jean turned and disappeared inside the limestone cave.

"Let me know if you need any help," Louise called after them.

"Okay," came Jean's hollow-sounding voice.

Louise looked around the woods, and to the mound of tailings heaped directly on top of the limestone cavern.

Five minutes went by, with Louise still keeping a sharp lookout. She saw no one, but suddenly as she again glanced upward, her heart froze. The piled-up tailings were starting to shift and trickle down.

"A landslide's starting!" Louise gasped.

In no time the tailings would cover the mouth of the cave and escape would be cut off for the girls inside!

"Jean! Janet!" she screamed wildly. "Come back! Quick! You'll be buried alive!"

At first there was no answer and Louise kept on yelling louder and louder. Finally the other two girls called back. She was relieved, but wondered fearfully if they could make it in time.

"Hurry!" she cried desperately.

"We're coming!" she heard Jean shout.

Suddenly there was a tremendous rumble, as a mass of earth and stones began pouring down.

Jean dashed from the cave just in time. A split second later tons of earth and rocks fell directly in front of the opening.

Louise and Jean had got out of the way of the avalanche, confident that Janet was behind them. When they stopped at a safe distance and looked back, the sisters did not see their friend. They stared at each other in horror.

"Janet! She—she's trapped—inside the cave!" Louise exclaimed in panic.

Quickly she turned and ran back, with Jean at her heels. The landslide had stopped now, and desperately the sisters began to claw at the tailings with their fingers. It soon became evident that their endeavours were in vain.

"Help!" Louise cried out. Jean took up the distress call.

Suddenly a man's husky voice boomed out, "Where are you?"

"At the limestone cave!" Jean yelled at the top of her voice.

Within a few seconds a man appeared through the woods. Louise and Jean gaped in astonishment, then cried out, "Dusty Hooper! Thank goodness!"

"What's wrong?" he asked.

Quickly Jean explained. "And we can't make any headway," she concluded, almost in tears, but still digging with her hands into the debris.

"Of course not," Dusty said with authority. "One of you run down to my truck and bring shovels. I'll do what I can here in the meantime."

Louise sped off, as the trucker used his large hands and the heels of his shoes to clear away the debris. By the time Louise returned, he and Jean together had made little progress because fresh earth kept falling down and covering the hole.

"Oh, what can we do?" Louise cried woefully. "How can we ever reach Janet?"

## CHAPTER X

# The Mysterious Date

"There's only one way that I know of to hold off this landslide," Dusty Hooper spoke up. "I'll prop myself against this hill of tailings and try to keep the dirt from falling while you dig."

He leaned face forward against the landslide, his arms raised above his head, his feet spread wide apart. Dusty instructed the girls to dig in the space between his knees.

"A hole just large enough to crawl through."

Louise and Jean started shovelling, quickly but carefully. This time they had more success, with Dusty's two hundred pounds holding the sliding earth in place.

"How's it coming?" he called, unable to see what they were doing.

"All right," Louise replied breathlessly, emptying a shovelful of dirt and stones.

In a few minutes the sisters cried out that they had broken through to the cave. Jean began calling, "Janet! Janet!"

To the girls' dismay there was no answer. They closed their eyes for a moment as if to shut out the awful thoughts which raced through their minds. Then Louise, fighting down panic, said, "Dusty, do you have a flashlight?"

"In my hip pocket."

Louise removed the light and crawled cautiously through the hole. In a few seconds she found Janet lying on the floor of the cave, unconscious.

"At least she's alive!" Louise thought.

Grasping her friend by the shoulders, she dragged her to the opening.

"I'll need help," she called to Jean.

Her sister crept through. She grasped Janet's ankles and began pushing the unconscious girl. Louise pulled her. The Danas held their breath, hoping there would not be another cave-in before they could get Janet outside. Luck was with them and they emerged safely.

The fresh air revived Janet almost instantly. Louise and Jean insisted that she rest for a few minutes.

As Dusty started to get up, Jean said quickly, "Oh, please don't move, Dusty. I want to go back into the cave and see if anyone else is trapped."

She did not add that she also wanted to take a

quick look for the chest of nuggets which Ying Mee might have buried there.

"Do be careful!" Louise begged.

"I will," Jean promised, and pulled herself back inside.

Dusty's large flashlight had a powerful beam and illuminated the gloomy interior very well. As Jean beamed the light around, she discovered that the cave was a rather deep one, narrowing toward the back. No one was in it.

The young sleuth now noticed that the cave consisted entirely of limestone, and afforded no good hiding places for a chest. Jean started back toward the entrance.

By the time she reached the outside, Jean found Janet fully recovered, though suffering a bit from shock because of her experience. She requested that they return to the motel at once, and the Danas agreed.

"I'll drive you all to your car," Dusty offered. "You girls walked a good distance from it."

Louise explained that they were hunting for the harmonica player, but had not found him, or any cabin in which he might live.

"If I ever come across him, I'll tell him to get in touch with you," Dusty promised.

"Thank you," said Janet. "And thank you for helping to save my life."

"I don't know what we would have done without you, Dusty," Louise added. "We were about at our wit's end."

The genial truck driver grinned. "Any time I can save a lady, I hope I'll hear the call for help. But I must admit this is the first time in my life I ever held back a landslide!"

Janet had time for a short nap before supper and awoke refreshed. Meanwhile, the Danas had telephoned Aunt Carol Reed and talked with her, then Aunt Harriet. The women had nothing to report about any clues concerning either Major Williams or Basil Tripley.

"The police haven't found a trace of that thief," Miss Dana went on, "and the ring hasn't turned up yet in any pawnshops or other likely places. We've heard nothing from Janet's mother, either. It's a shame about her father. Oh, I hope there'll be a turn for the better in both mysteries soon."

Louise and Jean related what little news they had but said the three girls were far from being discouraged.

"Some clue is bound to pay off," Louise declared.

The girls enjoyed dinner at a nearby restaurant, then returned to the motel. Early that evening Jean was summoned to the lobby telephone. Thinking the call was probably from the police chief, she was amazed to hear a young man's nasal voice on the line. "Jean Dana?"

"Yes."

"How are you, kid?"

Jean froze. "Who is this?" she demanded.

"I'll tell you later," the voice said, "if you want to pay for some information I have."

"That all depends on what it is," Jean said icily.

The young man went on to say that he had heard Jean and a couple of her girl friends were looking for an "old guy who played the harmonica."

"Go on," Jean prodded him.

"Well, are you?"

"Sort of," she admitted. "Is your information about him?"

"Well, I know where he is. Suppose you meet me in fifteen minutes downtown in front of the hotel. Bring your pocketbook with a fat wallet in it. I've got a hot tip, but as I said, it'll cost you money."

Jean thought fast. Was the young man telling the truth or was this some kind of hoax? She had been warned many times by the police to beware of anyone who demanded money in exchange for information, no matter how helpful it might be.

Suddenly another thought came to the young sleuth. The voice was vaguely familiar. Perhaps the caller was Hep Delaney, the insolent high school boy at the musical instrument counter in the Jackson shop!

"Well, how about it, sweetie?" the speaker asked.

"I—I'd certainly like to get the information," Jean answered, pretending to be hesitant, "but it would be most inconvenient for me to leave here this evening. How about your coming up to the motel? I'll meet you in the lobby, or out in front if you prefer."

"You ought to meet *me*. I'm the one with the information," the voice replied.

"I'm terribly sorry, but you'll have to come here," Jean insisted.

"Well, all right," the stranger conceded. "I'll be up to your place in a few minutes. Meet me in front, and don't bring your pals with you."

Jean hurried back to the girls and told them about the telephone conversation. "I'm sure he was Hep Delaney," she said, "although he tried to disguise his voice."

"Oh, maybe not," Janet said hopefully. "Let's do just what he asks. Only, how much do you think we should pay him?"

"He certainly won't get paid one nickel until he proves what he's going to tell me," Jean said determinedly. "But I have a strong hunch he won't show up."

Her prediction turned out to be true. Although she walked up and down in front of the motel for nearly an hour, no one appeared. She returned to the lower level, where Louise and Janet were seated in comfortable lawn chairs near the swimming pool.

"Did you get the information?" Janet asked excitedly.

Jean shook her head. "No one came. I thought all along it was a hoax."

"But perhaps not," said Janet sadly. "The person who called you might have been frightened off. Oh, dear, maybe we've missed a good clue to where the Major is!"

The Danas could not agree, since they were convinced the telephone caller was playing a practical joke, but felt sorry for Janet.

"I have a suggestion," said Louise. "Jean, why don't you call up Hep Delaney at his house and accuse him of breaking a date? If he's the guilty one, maybe you can catch him off guard."

Jean gladly accepted the assignment. "I'll put on a good act!"

She rushed up to the lobby telephone, looked up the number in the directory, and dialed the call. Hep himself answered the phone. Jean, in an almost sobbing voice, accused, "You broke the date with me at the motel."

As Louise had predicted, Hep fell into the trap.

"So you found out who was calling. Well, can't you take a joke? For Pete's sake, what kind of girls are you? I thought you were smart. You really are dumb. I haven't got any information about your old man." He laughed uproariously, then hung up.

Jean was grinning broadly herself. When she relayed the conversation, Janet jumped from her chair and hugged both Louise and Jean. "You are the most amazing people in the world," she said. "I just love you both to pieces."

Everyone else had left the grounds of the motel and the girls felt it safe to talk, in whispers at least, about the buried chest of nuggets. They tried to figure out possible hiding places.

"Perhaps under some hearthstone," Janet ventured a guess.

Louise had an idea also. "There were covered wagons around here back in those days. Maybe Ying Mee put the nuggets into one which he felt might never be used again but would remain intact—at least until after Franklin Reed found the treasure."

"I'm inclined to think," said Jean, "that Ying Mee hid the chest some place in one of their Chinatowns around here—for instance, in a joss house."

The girls finally decided that they should take each town separately and search among the ruins of buildings in the Chinese quarters. "Let's begin with the places where the largest groups of Chinese lived," Louise suggested.

Eager to make an early start on their search, the three sleuths soon went to bed. It seemed to all of them as if their eyes had barely closed when they were awakened by sounds outside the windows overlooking the patio.

Someone was playing a harmonica, and playing it very well!

Louise and Jean jumped from their beds, grabbed robes, and dashed outside.

## CHAPTER XI

# The Joss House

ON THE porch outside their doors the Dana girls met Janet. Her eyes were darting from one spot to another excitedly.

"You heard it too?" she said. "The harmonica player! Do you suppose it could be the Major?"

"I did think so at first, but not now," Louise responded. "Tell you about it later."

Jean said, "You girls run that way, I'll go the other." She indicated the exit from the parking lot which went around one end of the building to the area in front of the motel. Louise and Janet darted off. Jean herself rushed along the porch in the other direction and up a slope at the far end.

No one was in sight, but as the girls neared the upper level, they all heard a motor being started. As they reached the highway, Louise caught a glimpse of a young man pulling away in a car.

*Hep Delaney!*

"He was the one playing the harmonica," Louise said. "I thought so. He played a wrong note in that melody he was blowing."

Janet giggled nervously. "I don't know whether to feel better or worse. But even though we did not find the Major, I'm glad Hep Delaney and his hoax were discovered."

The girls returned to their rooms and once more fell asleep. The following morning, Sunday, the girls went to church, then had dinner. While eating they decided which town to investigate first.

Louise suggested Fiddletown. "Many Chinese were there, and I understand the ruins of a joss house are still standing."

"How in the world did a town ever get that name?" Jean asked with a smile.

Louise, who had been reading about the area, replied, "The place was settled by people from Missouri. They loved to play fiddles, dance, and have a good time. Once a judge from there went to San Francisco and registered at a hotel. When he signed Fiddletown after his name, people laughed at him.

"He was so embarrassed that when he got back home he announced that he was going to change the town's name. So it was called Oleta for a while. But a group from San Francisco, the very town in which the judge had been laughed at, requested the local people to have the interesting original name restored. So Fiddletown it is."

"Very quaint," said Jean. "Well, let's get started."

Jean again drove and took Highway 49 north until she came to Plymouth, then turned to the right. Some distance beyond was Fiddletown, where she parked on the small town's main street. The girls strolled around, taking particular note of the old adobe structures built by the Chinese.

"Isn't it amazing how parts of them have stood up all this time," Louise remarked. "They're made of only mud."

Janet nodded. "Some of them were forts erected by the Chinese to protect themselves against Mexican bandits who came up here on raids."

The girls walked on, and presently stopped in front of another adobe building onto which someone had attached a sign, reading:

*House of Worship of the Chinese*
*Who Helped Build Fiddletown*

"Let's investigate and see if by any chance the chest of nuggets is hidden here," Jean proposed.

As she was about to enter, a young couple walked up to the joss house. The Danas, not wishing to divulge their secret to the strangers, pretended to be only sightseeing.

The newcomers were friendly and talkative. They introduced themselves as Mr. and Mrs. Dodd.

"Jack Spratt and his wife," thought Jean, noting the overthin husband and overplump wife.

The Dodds claimed to be well versed in Amador County lore and history and offered to answer any questions the girls might have.

Smiling, Louise said, "Thank you. I guess we're just like all other sightseers, wondering how much buried gold is still in the ground."

Mr. Dodd replied instantly. "Not very much, if any, in Fiddletown. Every inch of this place has been dug up or tested for high-grader's gold."

"High-grader's gold?" Jean repeated.

"That's about the only kind which was hidden. There were quite a few miners who were not absolutely honest. They devised all sorts of ways of taking gold out of the mines they were working, and secreting it on their persons to avoid turning it in to their bosses."

"You say in the mines," said Louise. "Then the term 'high-graders' wouldn't apply to a man working on his own and panning gold."

"No. But many of those old-timers had partners who didn't share their diggings with them fair and square. Sometimes they hid the stuff. But I'm sure all of it around here has been dug up by this time."

The three girls looked at one another, the same

discouraging thought in all their minds. If Ying Mee had buried his treasure in the joss house or anywhere else around Fiddletown, there was little doubt it already had been found!

Trying to be nonchalant in her next question, Louise asked the Dodds if they had ever heard of any unusual nuggets having been dug up.

"Oh, yes," Mrs. Dodd replied immediately. "Why, there's not a town around here that can't tell you a story of strangely shaped nuggets. One looked like a statue of Buddha, another like a bowl of rice."

As the woman paused, the girls waited tensely wondering if she would mention that one of the nuggets was in the shape of a rocker.

Her husband took up the story. "Evelyn, do you remember that story we heard over in what used to be called Hangman's Gulch?"

Mrs. Dodd laughed. "Oh, yes, I remember." Turning to the girls, she said, "Listen to this one: A Chinese teapot was once found—"

The girls listened intently as the woman continued, "I understand it was an exquisite teapot. Anyhow, in it was a small fortune in nuggets. And, nestled right in among them, was a beautiful piece of jade."

"Jade?" Jean asked, puzzled. "Did they find jade around here?"

"Not that kind of jade," Mr. Dodd answered.

"The piece in the teapot probably had been brought from China. Anyway, it added to the value of the contents of the teapot. Whoever the lucky finder was, I'll bet he was able to retire!"

The Dodds had other stories to tell about caches of gold having been found. But they finished their narratives without mentioning that any contained a nugget which had been hammered into the shape of a miner's rocker.

The Danas felt a sense of relief. There was still a ray of hope that Ying Mee's treasure was intact!

Louise asked the Dodds if in their research about the Forty-niners they had ever come across the name Ying Mee. At first neither of them could recall the name, then suddenly Mr. Dodd hit the palm of one hand with his fist.

"I remember! In looking over some old records of either the Wells Fargo or Adams Company I saw the name Ying Mee in a list of Forty-niners who had sold gold to those companies."

As the girls exchanged excited glances, Mrs. Dodd put in, "You know back in those days there weren't any banks in Amador County, so the pony express companies acted as bankers and delivered the gold to the United States Government."

"California wasn't a state at that time," Jean said. "I read in an old diary of a homesick miner that he wished he could get back to the United States! Nowadays that seems funny, doesn't it?"

"Sure does." Mr. Dodd chuckled, adding, "A tremendous amount of gold was shipped from here to the mint in Philadelphia."

Janet spoke up. "I seem to remember the Major telling me that in a hundred-year period two billion dollars' worth was shipped out of here!"

"That's amazing!" Louise exclaimed.

The three girls asked further questions, and Janet showed the Dodds the photograph of Major Williams. But the couple could give them no further help on either Ying Mee or Janet's grandfather.

"If you're interested in the old Chinese miners, you should make some inquiries in Drytown, Ione, and several other places," Mr. Dodd advised. "There were a good many of the Orientals here. In one mining camp alone, out of the eight thousand inhabitants, two thousand of them were Chinese."

The Dodds said good-by and wished the girls luck.

"Thank you very much for all your information," Jean spoke up.

Since there probably was no chance of locating the Reed treasure in Fiddletown, she was eager to go to another spot. The girls walked to their car, got in, and started back toward Plymouth.

"I have a strong hunch we're wasting our time," Louise spoke up. "From the letters I read at Aunt Carol's, I gather that Ying Mee was a very bright person. I'm sure he never would have hidden the chest of nuggets in a place where later it could be claimed by the owner of the property."

"What kind of a place would that be?" Janet asked.

"Well, I don't know exactly," Louise answered. "But I think he would have buried the chest out of doors in some spot not likely ever to become private property or to have a building erected over it."

"That really narrows our search," Jean said with a sigh. "There's not much left except the area along the public roads."

The girls reached Plymouth and Jean turned south onto Highway 49. She continued on to Amador City. Arriving at the outskirts, she descended a hill that led to the centre of town, then made a sharp turn to the right and started up another hill. Suddenly the girls were horrified to see a truck careening down directly toward them.

"That truck must be out of control!" Janet shrieked. "It'll hit us!"

## CHAPTER XII

# Volcano Clue

TENSE moments followed as the heavy truck continued its pell-mell flight down the hill. Jean realized that her only chance to get out of the way was to back up—and fast.

She swung the lever into reverse and the car shot backward. Worried that the driver of the truck might manage to turn the corner, Jean kept going up the other hill.

"He'll have to stop before he gets very far on this slope," she thought.

When Jean decided she was a safe enough distance away, she stopped. At that very moment the truck reached the foot of the hill, shot across the road, narrowly missing a brick building, and disappeared from view.

"It's gone into the cemetery!" Janet exclaimed.

"We must go help the driver," Louise added.

Jean drove to the foot of the hill, rounded the corner, and parked a short distance from Mr. Fish's museum. The girls climbed out and raced back into the cemetery. The truck, which had gone up an incline, had stopped just short of a tombstone. The driver was groggily climbing from the cab.

"Dusty Hooper!" Louise cried out.

She started to run and soon reached the man's side. "Oh, Dusty, are you hurt?" she asked, as the other girls rushed up.

The trucker gave them a wan smile. "I guess I'm more frightened than hurt," he said shakily. "My brakes didn't hold coming down that hill. I was on my way to a garage to have the truck put in shape for tomorrow. Whew! I don't want that experience again!"

"Why don't you sit down here for a little while until you relax?" Louise suggested kindly, indicating a grassy patch.

Dusty needed no urging. He dropped to the ground and shook his head as if to clear his brain. But within a few minutes he arose and said he must telephone the manager of his company.

He managed a grin. "I imagine the town fathers around here wouldn't exactly appreciate a truck in their cemetery!"

As he walked into a store in a nearby old brick

building, the girls went up the road to the Gold Rush Museum.

Mr. Frank Fish came to greet them. His eyes twinkling, he asked, "Did you come to see my tottering Indian again?"

The girls laughed, then Louise said, "We're not having much luck finding what we're looking for. We wonder if we might rent your metal detector."

"Yes, if you'll take good care of it. And I hope you'll find a million with it!" the genial curator said. He went to get the detector and returned shortly with the device.

He had just finished instructing the girls how to use it when the door of the museum opened and Dusty strode in. He nodded to Mr. Fish, then said excitedly to the girls, "Say, a man just stopped for a moment in that store where I was. While he was making a purchase and waiting for change, he mentioned seeing a very unusual character in the woods. The man had white hair and a long white beard."

"That must be the man you saw!" Jean said to Louise.

Dusty went on, "The old man said he was up in Mother Lode country on a very strange errand. He wasn't looking for nuggets of gold like most people are—he was trying to find a cave in which a large quantity of gold had been hidden."

Janet and the Danas were listening intently.

Dusty continued, "This stranger at the store said the old man told him that some ancient people called Lemurians had hidden a fabulous fortune there. Boy, would I like to find it!"

"Where is this stranger you saw?" Janet asked excitedly. "I want to talk to him."

"He said he was in a hurry and drove off," Dusty replied, "but I thought you'd like the information, so I came to give it to you."

"Oh, thank you!" Janet said. Turning to the Danas, she added, "That old man with the white beard had the same idea as the Major! He may even have met him."

Dusty smiled. "I sure wish you luck. I'd say the place to hunt for him is around Volcano. But don't go into the woods today. It's too late—it'll soon be dark."

The girls, though eager to start another search, knew the advice was wise. They said good-by to Dusty and Mr. Fish, and drove to the motel.

The following morning they set off for Volcano, taking the direct route from Jackson.

"What glorious and picturesque country this is!" Louise exclaimed admiringly, after they had gone up and down wooded hills and through scenic open spaces.

"Where do you think we should begin our search for the bearded man?" Janet asked, eager to get started.

"At the next woody spot," Louise answered.

The girls stopped several times, calling for Major Williams, for the white-bearded man, even for the harmonica player. Their efforts brought no response, and finally they set off on the last part of their trip to Volcano.

When they reached it, the young travellers were instantly charmed by the quaint village. There was an air of peace about it which they had not found in the other towns they had visited.

"Where shall we start our inquiries?" Janet asked.

Jean chuckled. "I won't be able to do anything until I have lunch," she said.

The car was parked and the girls strolled along the main street. They passed an old-time two-balconied hotel, called the St. George, the stone ruins of a general store, a Wells Fargo Agency, a museum, gift shop, and tearoom.

"Oh, look!" Louise exclaimed, pointing to a small wooden building the size of a one-car garage. "There's a cannon inside, behind the wire front!"

The three girls gazed within, then read the sign tacked to the wire.

"This cannon was named after Abraham Lincoln," Jean remarked. "That's why it's called 'Old Abe.'"

The sign revealed that the cannon was a relic of the Civil War when sentiments ran high in Volcano between sympathizers for the North and those for the South. The Unionist group was called the Volcano Blues, while the Confederate sympathizers were known as the Knights of the Gold Circle.

"Surely these people weren't fighting battles way out here!" Janet remarked.

"No," said Louise. "But a great deal of gold was shipped from here for the use of the Northerners, and of course the Southern sympathizers wanted it to go to the Confederacy."

Janet and the Danas learned that the cannon had been forged in South Boston, bought in San Francisco by the Volcano Blues, sent by boat to Sacramento, and then by freight wagon to Jackson.

Suddenly the girls smiled, and Jean remarked, "What a clever ruse those Northerners played! They brought the cannon from Jackson to Volcano in a hearse so the Southerners wouldn't suspect."

The sign on the wire fence also stated that the local blacksmith had secretly put the cannon into firing condition. At an appropriate moment, when the Knights of the Gold Circle were marching up the street to take charge of the gold shipments, the Northern sympathizers brought the cannon from hiding and set it in the middle of the road.

"That did the trick!" Jean said, chuckling. "Not a shot was fired! The Southerners gave up and there was no further trouble in the town."

The girls entered the Jug and Rose Tearoom. Since it was late for the lunch hour, the place was only partially filled. The Danas decided that while eating, they would ask the owner some questions which might help them in their search.

They were greeted by a pleasant, sparkling-eyed woman who introduced herself as Mrs. Thebaut, co-owner of the restaurant. They ordered homemade vegetable soup, which proved to be delectable, bulging, tasty, chicken-salad sandwiches, and homemade apple pie.

Mrs. Thebaut handed the girls folded tea menu cards. Jean, upon looking at hers, exclaimed, "I never heard of so many kinds of tea in my life. There are actually eighteen varieties here!"

She herself chose "constant comment." Louise decided on jasmine, and Janet took "king's garden."

As they were eating the apple pie, Mrs. Thebaut walked over and said, "Here comes Mr. Wintle, another co-owner with my husband and me. He is one of the people from a foreign land who fell in love with Volcano and never left here. He's a water-colour artist from South Africa, and is the official artist of the Mother Lode country. Later you must go over to the gift shop and see some of his work."

She called Mr. Wintle over to the table. He was

slender and alert-looking, and proved to be a store-house of information on Mother Lode country, as did Mrs. Thebaut. The girls were fascinated with their stories, especially the one about two private schools in Volcano founded in 1855. One was Miss Hoyt's Female Seminary, devoted to the pursuits of art, the other a school for boys run by her brother. Both tried to lift the tastes of the mine owners' children to a high level.

"There were other people around here quite different from the miners," Mrs. Thebaut said. "The Mi-wok Indians, for instance. One place you girls must visit is the great Indian Rock between here and Pine Grove where the women came to grind the nuts and berries which they gathered."

"The Mi-wok Indians were not noted for their industriousness," Mr. Wintle put in. "There are some amusing stories of how they waited for the squirrels to gather the harvest of nuts, then actually stole them."

"But the poor squirrels! What did they do?" Janet asked.

Mrs. Thebaut chuckled. "They probably went to a safer place."

The conversation finally got around to the mysterious harmonica player in the woods. "I wonder if we'll ever find him?" said Louise.

As she finished speaking, a woman seated with a group of friends at another table looked startled.

She got up and came over to the girls' table.

"I wonder if I could help you," she said. "I'm Mrs. Ernest. Yesterday a strange thing happened. I took my children and a couple of their friends on a picnic in the woods a little way out of town. Suddenly we heard what sounded like a harmonica being played. We looked all around but could see no one.

"Then I told the children that when I was a little girl my father had told me a story about a 'harmonica' bird. I assumed there was no such thing, but immediately the children wanted to go hunting for the bird. To please them, we tramped a short distance through the woods.

"Suddenly, ahead of us, in a little clearing, we were startled by seeing two men, one old, the other younger, in a tussle. The older one had a large harmonica. The younger man was trying to grab it."

"Did he succeed?" Louise asked.

"No. The children and I yelled and the young man ran away. The older one went off too, in a different direction, and we didn't see either of them again," the woman concluded.

"Please tell us more about the men," Jean begged.

Mrs. Ernest said she knew nothing else, except that the older man was white-haired. "The other, I'd judge, was about thirty years old."

"Did the old man have a white beard?" Louise inquired.

"No. He had snow-white hair, but no beard."

Janet was already opening her purse. Excitedly she withdrew the picture of Major Williams. Showing it to Mrs. Ernest, she asked, "Was this the man?"

## CHAPTER XIII

# Frog Jumping

MRS. ERNEST studied the photograph of Major Williams intently. Finally she handed it back.

"I'm sorry, but I realize I was not close enough to either of the men to identify them. All I can tell you is that the older one was tall and very straight. The younger one wore a large-brimmed hat, was of medium height, slender, and stoop-shouldered."

Janet and the Danas were disappointed. Louise spoke up, "Could you tell us, Mrs. Ernest, your exact location when you saw the men?"

"Oh, I can do that easily," the woman answered. "Take the road from here toward Sutter Creek. About two miles out of town you'll come to a wooded section where a mountain stream comes tumbling down a canyon. On your left, straight ahead and about a hundred yards from the road is the spot where the attempted robbery occurred."

The girls, eager to get to the place, arose and

quickly thanked Mrs. Ernest, Mrs. Thebaut, and Mr. Wintle for their interesting data on the locale. The three wished Janet, Louise, and Jean good luck, as they waved good-by from the doorway.

In a short time Louise, who was driving, came to the rushing mountain stream. "I'd sure like to pan that sometime!" she said eagerly.

Jean smiled. "I agree. After we get the mysteries solved, we ought to stay around here awhile and dig up some gold."

Janet's eyes twinkled. "If you find a chest of nuggets, you won't have to work for the rest of your lives!"

Louise parked and the girls set off through the woods on the left side of the road. What a glorious sight it was! Despite the fact that their minds were on the unsolved mysteries, they could not help but notice the tall, stately madroña trees with their crowns of ripening berries in rust-tinted jackets; the brilliant red-and-orange foliage of the dogwoods with clusters of crimson fruit; the wild-rose bushes scattered through the open areas, their prickly stems hung with seed pods which looked like miniature ripe apples.

"Those are the rose hips," Janet told them, pointing to the pods. "Have you ever eaten any?"

"No," the Danas replied.

"Then you've missed a treat," Janet told them. "The rose hips are tart, but delicious."

Presently the girls reached the little clearing about which Mrs. Ernest had told them. "Look!" Jean exclaimed. "Here are two sets of footprints!"

"And one of them," Louise added excitedly, "is exactly like the set we saw the other day!"

"The question is," Jean said, after studying both sets, "which one belongs to the old man and which to the younger."

Janet looked at first one sister, then the other. "You're detectives." She grinned. "You ought to be able to figure that out."

"Well," said Louise, thinking aloud, "let's assume that the younger man is stronger and is the one who threw that limb at us. If so, these footprints belong to him. And, by the way, why was he following us the other day?"

"Maybe," Jean took up the train of thought, "the younger man has some reason for trying to keep us away from the older man."

Janet was curious, and even ventured a guess herself. "It's because the old man is in hiding!"

"Could be," Jean replied. "The fact that the old man ran away from Mrs. Ernest and the children makes your idea very plausible."

"And that old man could be the Major!" Janet said, walking about nervously. "Let's follow his footprints!"

They led to the stream, then along its bank. Presently the girls could see a small cabin.

"Do you suppose he lives there?" Janet asked in a whisper. "If he's hiding, maybe we should surround the cabin and surprise him, so he can't get away."

Louise and Jean smiled. "Janet, you're getting to be a real sleuth!" Louise said with a low chuckle.

As the girls considered separating, they suddenly became aware of voices. They stopped. A man and a boy were talking on the far side of the cabin.

"I tell you it won't make any difference," the man was saying.

"Aw, Pa, why don't you give me a chance?" the boy whined.

The three girls huddled together. "Let's see what they're doing before they find out we're here," Louise proposed.

She felt that they should circle the cabin as they approached. When the others agreed, Louise herself took the left side near the stream, while Jean, trailed by Janet, sneaked up on the right. As all three girls hid behind some low-growing willow trees, they gasped in amazement.

A rugged-looking man and a boy of about twelve were watching a giant frog give great leaps here and there. Suddenly the boy pounced on the fourteen-inch-long frog and held him, while his father took a tape from his pocket and measured the distance of the jumps.

Pa shook his head. "No good. Too crooked."

The boy gently stroked the frog and said, "Beauty, you *got* to do better than that. What's the matter today? Didn't you get enough sleep last night?"

The girls could hardly keep from giggling. The entertainment was so fascinating they completely forgot they had come to see if an old man was hiding in the cabin.

"We'll try again," said Pa. "Set 'er down."

This time the frog jumped somewhat greater distances than before, but in a triangular direction. Both the man and the boy groaned.

"Beauty got right back where she started from," Pa said in disgust.

"But she did jump farther," the boy said encouragingly.

Pa measured the distance. Then he said, "One more try, Beauty. If you don't behave this time, you're goin' to put yourself out of the runnin'."

He himself took Beauty and set her on the ground. He stomped the earth behind her, which made Beauty leap high and far. "That's more like it," he said.

As he measured the distance, Beauty jumped back toward the boy. Pa flung the tape measure on the ground.

"Can I try my jumping trough now?" the boy asked.

"All right, Tim."

As Pa held the frog, Tim dashed to the side of the cabin and dragged out a very long board. A two-foot-high fencing of slats and chicken wire had been nailed onto the long sides. The ends were open.

"So that's the jumping trough," the girls thought. "What's Tim going to do with it?"

"The record's sixteen feet, two inches for a frog jump," said Pa. "Now, Beauty," he went on, setting her down at one end of the trough, "see if you can come near that record."

"She'll be allowed three jumps in the contest," Tim spoke up. "This trough is twenty feet long."

The hidden girls had seated themselves on the ground to watch the jumping. Louise was not far from the end of the trough.

Intently she gazed at Beauty. The frog leaped up, came down, sprang again, and landed. Then, as if inspired, Beauty gave a tremendous jump forward, her hind legs spread out behind her. She pulled them in just in time before landing.

Tim gave a whoop of joy. "She's beaten the record!" he cried.

His exclamation apparently frightened Beauty, who gave another tremendous jump, which took her far beyond the end of the trough. She turned to the left, and made another high leap.

*She was aimed directly toward Louise's face!*

"Catch Beauty! She's worth a lot of money!" Pa cried frantically.

By this time Jean and Janet, realizing that Louise had been spotted, hurried from their hiding place and joined in the endeavour to capture the frog.

They stooped, missed, dashed hither and yon, with Beauty seemingly enjoying the game, and showing no intention of giving up.

"You come back here, you old frog!" Pa cried angrily.

Beauty made one final leap toward freedom, landing at the very edge of the water. Jean swooped down and caught her with both hands before she could enter the stream. As the girl gazed at her captive's face, she smiled, thinking Beauty was anything but beautiful!

Jean turned toward Pa. "You said that Beauty is worth a lot of money. How much?"

His answer stunned the girls. "Eight hundred dollars."

## CHAPTER XIV

# A Strange Inquiry

BEFORE answering Jean's question as to why Beauty was so valuable, the man introduced himself as Mr. Salter and his son as Tim. He said the two of them spent a great deal of time at the cabin because they liked to fish and "rough it" in the open. During the school year they lived in Sacramento but came up to the woods at every opportunity.

"Oh, yes," Pa Salter went on. "You asked me why Beauty is worth eight hundred dollars. That's because she's going to win the broad-jumping contest down at Angels Camp. There's a prize of eight hundred dollars to any frog who can beat the record."

"And Beauty jumped farther than that a few minutes ago!" Tim put in proudly.

Louise said she was interested to know more

about the frog-jumping contest, so the Salters obligingly explained.

"It started way back in 1865," Pa said. "Then for a while they didn't have the contests. But in 1928 the citizens of Angels Camp decided to hold the event again."

"You ought to see it!" Tim exclaimed. "Boy, is that place crowded! Why, ten thousand people come to the grandstand in the fairgrounds to watch the frogs."

Mr. Salter said that the townspeople dress up like the Forty-niners. A platform, thirty-two by forty-eight feet, is erected. This is the jumping arena, where a panel of comic-serious judges in frock coats and top hats preside.

"The frogs appear on a Saturday for the elimination rounds," Pa Salter went on. "The top ten make the finals."

"I noticed," said Jean, "that you were worried by Beauty's not jumping in a straight line."

"That's right," Pa replied. "On the platform there's painted a set of three circles like on a target. The frog is placed on the bull's-eye and is allowed three jumps. Of course everyone hopes he'll jump in a straight line, because the frog who ends up the farthest from the bull's-eye is the winner of the contest."

Tim grinned. "We're starting early this year on Beauty and with my gadget here we'll teach her to jump in a straight line and win that big money!"

"Well, I certainly wish you luck," said Louise, and the other two girls echoed her best wishes.

Suddenly Pa Salter began to laugh. "You know, the study of frogs is real interesting. For one thing, they're sensitive to gravity, and for this reason they keep their heads as high as they can. Another thing: If the water they live in is warmer than the air, most of the frogs' bodies are in the water. But if the water is colder than the air, the frogs are likely to be sitting on a rock in the sunshine."

Tim went on to say that a frog swallows its food alive. "If whatever he swallows gets too lively, the old frog has a digestive 'hot foot.' Say, Pa, we might use that. How about giving Beauty a live grasshopper just before her turn in the competition? It sure might make her jump far."

"And it might drive her crazy and make her go in circles!" his father replied.

Everyone laughed, then the girls became serious. Louise said they would like to ask Mr. Salter and his son a few questions.

"We're here in the woods trying to find three different men," she explained. "One looks like an old-time miner with snow-white hair and a long beard. Another is a tall, slender, clean-shaven, elderly man with white hair. The third is a man in his thirties. He's about medium height and very skinny. Have you seen any of these men?"

Pa Salter and his son looked at each other for several seconds before the man said, "Why do you want to know if we've seen them?"

The girls were not sure how much of the mystery they should divulge. Finally Jean spoke up. "We saw the old bearded man one day over at Jackson Gate. We figured he lives around here and might have seen the other old man and even talked with him."

Mr. Salter looked at the ground, made a little hole with the toe of his boot, then said, "You girls got something up your sleeves. I think you better tell me about it before I answer any more questions."

Janet, feeling that the Salters did have some information but for reasons of their own did not want to give it, pretended to pout. "You're forgetting we saved your valued Beauty for you. Don't you think you might at least answer a few questions for us?"

"I guess you're right," Pa Salter replied. "I can't tell you anything about the two old men you're looking for, but that young man—he must be the same one who was here. And two of you must be the girls he was asking about. Is your name Dana?"

The sisters were amazed by his question. They introduced themselves and Janet, then Louise asked, "Who was the young man?"

"He didn't give his name," Pa Salter replied. "He was kind of a queer duck. He asked Tim and me not to tell anyone he's been inquiring about you."

"What did he look like?" Jean asked.

Tim spoke up. "He was just like you said, medium height and awful skinny. He had light hair —and boy, was it long and stringy!"

The Danas and Janet tried not to show any undue interest, but the description exactly fitted the suspected thief, Basil Tripley! Speculations about him raced through their minds. What was he doing in this area—hiding from the authorities?

Had he perhaps followed Louise and Jean from Sacramento? But why, since he surely surmised the theft of Louise's ring had been reported to the police and that authorities in the area would be on the alert for him?

"He may have another purpose," Louise reasoned, "such as finding out why we came to Mother Lode country!"

Jean was saying to herself, "I wonder if he could have found out about Ying Mee's buried treasure!"

All the girls were curious to learn if the young man who had come to the cabin was the same one who had tried to rob the elderly man of his valuable harmonica. Louise began to hunt for footprints like those the girls had followed the day

of the tree-limb incident. Presently, in a somewhat marshy spot, she found some.

"Were these made by the man you're talking
about?" she asked.

Pa Salter and his son walked over to look at
them. "I guess they were," the father replied.
"That's the direction the fellow came from."

Louise looked at her wrist watch. "We really
should be getting back," she said, as an excuse to
leave. She wanted to follow the footprints that
might belong to Basil Tripley.

Janet and the Danas said good-by and again
wished the Salters luck with Beauty. Then
quickly they followed the marks in the soil. Presently Jean remarked in a low voice, "You know,
the footprints of the older man we followed before led us near the Salters' cabin."

"Do you suppose the Salters never did see him,
or were they just not telling us they had?" Janet
asked.

"It's hard to say," Louise answered. "At first,
Pa and Tim acted as if they didn't want to answer
any questions at all."

"I'd like to return there sometime and really find
out if they ever met the Major," Janet said pen-
sively.

The girls hurried on. At one point they lost the
footprints completely and for a moment wondered
if the man had climbed a stalwart maple nearby

and was hiding above. But the tree had lost most of its yellow leaves and concealed no one.

The searchers went toward the road, and near it picked up the footprints again. They turned away from Volcano and were lost in the maze of tire tracks.

"I guess this means we'll have to give up the hunt," Jean said disgustedly. "But as soon as we get back to Volcano, I'm going to report our suspicions about Basil Tripley to the police."

"Yes, we should," Louise agreed.

The girls walked along the road toward their car. Janet looked so sad over their failure to get a clue to her grandfather that the Danas wondered how they might cheer her up.

"Anybody's feet hot and tired except mine?" Jean asked.

"Mine are," Janet replied.

"Then I have a suggestion," said Jean. "Let's wade in that wonderful mountain stream where we left our car."

The others heartily approved the suggestion, so as soon as they reached the little canyon, the girls took off their hiking shoes and socks, rolled up their jeans, and stepped into the cool, refreshing water.

"Oh, I feel better already," said Janet as she bent down to splash her wrists.

The three girls began to walk up the stream.

"Maybe if we look carefully we'll find some gold!" Jean suggested.

She and Janet at once began gazing intently at the rocks in the stream. But Louise kept looking upward admiringly at the lovely scene around them. Suddenly, as she turned, she saw a rock come hurtling through the air in their direction.

"Girls! Look out!" she shrieked, pointing.

## CHAPTER XV

# Metal-Detector Clicks

JEAN and Janet looked toward Louise, then upward. All three girls made a dash out of the way of the flying rock which landed with a tremendous splash directly in front of them.

"Someone threw that!" Jean sputtered angrily. "And I'll bet it was the same person who tried to hit us with the tree limb!"

The words were hardly out of her mouth when something white, which looked like a package, came whizzing through the air. The girls dodged the "package," which landed in a manzanita bush a short distance from them.

As Jean and Janet rushed over to see what it was, Louise continued to gaze upward. She hoped to get a glimpse of the person who had thrown the rock. But he was nowhere in sight, and she saw no movement among the bushes or trees to indicate that he was leaving the area.

"This isn't a package!" Jean cried out. "It's a stone with a paper tied around it!"

"Maybe it's a note," Louise called, her eyes still darting around the hillside.

A few seconds later Jean said, "That's exactly what it is."

The note was printed in pencil. It said:

*Notify the police and you will wish you never had!*

Janet looked alarmed. "Someone heard you girls talking about communicating with the police," she said.

Louise walked over to the other two girls and read the note herself. Giving her friends a big wink, she said in a loud voice, "This is very frightening. We will certainly think twice now about going to the police."

As she finished speaking, Louise wondered if the rock thrower had heard her. She was positive that he was either Basil Tripley or some friend of his.

"More than likely," she whispered to Jean and Janet, "Tripley sent this warning. That's all the more reason why we should go to the police."

Aloud she suggested to the other girls that they put on their shoes and socks and leave at once. They did this and started for the car.

When they were settled inside, Jean said, "I think instead of going direct to the authorities, we should go right back to the motel and notify the police secretly. If we do it from Volcano, Basil Tripley may find out about it."

The others agreed, so Louise drove immediately to their Jackson motel. From there, she talked to the local police chief and asked if a plainclothesman could be sent up to talk with her about a clue to a thief.

In a short time the detective arrived. He showed the girls his credentials, and listened in amazement to their story.

"A posse will be sent out right away to hunt for this Basil Tripley," he said. "We have already been informed he's a wanted thief."

The officer advised the girls to stay out of the woods for a time, in case the suspect was still roaming around. "He's apparently a dangerous individual."

The girls promised to be careful. After the officer had gone, they went back to the Danas' bedroom and discussed the subject fully.

"I suppose we should keep our sleuthing more secretive," Louise remarked.

"In this case it would be pretty hard." Jean objected. "How are we ever going to look for a buried chest of nuggets without asking for clues and working outdoors?"

"And how," Janet added, "can I ever find the Major without making some inquiries?"

Louise said she thought they had best pretend

they were not doing anything at all on the mysteries. "And right now let's change our clothes and go downtown to dinner."

It was a welcome diversion and put the girls in a more cheerful mood. When they returned to the Danas' room, Louise offered to read from the old diary she had purchased. Perhaps contained in its pages would be a clue to a good hiding place for a chest of nuggets!

Janet sprawled on one of the beds. Jean lounged in an armchair, while Louise sat in a straight chair and began to read.

"In this part the diarist is still in the covered-wagon train," she explained. "It says: 'Last night we got no sleep. After supper there was a stampede of buffalo right past us. It lasted for two whole hours and nearly wrekked our train.'"

"How horrible!" Janet exclaimed. "Can you imagine how many buffalo there must have been?"

"I'm sure I would have been scared silly," Jean commented.

Louise read on:

" 'Following the buffalo came a huge pack of wolves. They yelped and fought and a few stayed at our camp to annoy the horses. I have never heard anything more hideous than their howling.'"

"Ugh!" said Janet. "Please turn to the pages when that diarist was actually in Mother Lode country."

Louise turned several pages. Presently she began to chuckle. "Here's part of an old song by a miner who wasn't making out so well, I guess," she said.

" 'I've nothing but rags to my back
And my boots scarce hide my toes,
While my pants are patched with an
old flour sack
To jibe with the rest of my clothes.' "

The girls laughed, although they felt a tinge of sympathy for the men who had left their families, endured tremendous hardships to come to Mother Lode country, yet had found little or no gold. Page after page of the diary told anecdotes of daily life, but there seemed to be no clue to a hiding place which Ying Mee might have picked out to secrete his chest of nuggets.

Then suddenly Louise began to read a section which made both Janet and Jean sit up straight. It told how the men had worked in a river, digging some five feet down through the gravel to bedrock, where they had found a good quantity of gold in the cracks and clay. But this was an unusual procedure.

"Now that would have been a sensible place for Ying Mee to have put the chest," Janet remarked. "People rarely disturb rivers or smaller bodies of water."

"I think your hunch is a good one," said Jean. "But where in the world would we start? There are hundreds of little streams throughout Amador County."

At that moment a knock came on the door and the motel owner said that Janet was wanted on the phone. Her mother was calling. The girl hurried off.

When Janet returned, she announced excitedly that the police had picked up a new lead on the disappearance of Major Williams.

"They think he took a ship to Honolulu! A search is being made now in the Hawaiian Islands. Oh, I feel so much better. Do you realize that this is the first real clue the police have had?"

The Danas expressed their delight at the news, saying they hoped something certainly would come out of this. Both young sleuths were convinced they had a good lead themselves that Major Williams had come to Mother Lode country. But in view of Janet's announcement, they felt free now to concentrate on their own mystery.

The following morning the girls brought out maps and carefully studied the roads which the Forty-niners had travelled. They finally decided to use their rented metal detector along the road from Jackson to Sacramento.

Eager to start, they hurried downtown to breakfast, then set off on Highway 49 as far as Drytown.

Here they turned west onto Route 16, and presently Jean, at the wheel, parked the car.

"How shall we do this?" she asked. "Walk along both sides a little way, then drive on?"

Louise had a suggestion. "Suppose just one of us walks, while the other two follow in the car. We'll do one side of the road this morning and try the other side coming back."

"And take turns holding the metal detector," Janet added. The others nodded.

"I'd like to go first," said Jean.

She got out of the car, lifted the metal detector from the rear seat, and carried it to the side of the road. Then she adjusted the earphones and began to walk, carrying the detector. Presently Jean heard a slow, steady, loud background clicking.

Excitedly she looked at the meter needle. It was unmistakably advancing! In a moment she cried:

"The clicking's very loud now! The buried metal must be here!"

## CHAPTER XVI

# Identifying a Thief

THEIR hearts pounding in anticipation, Louise and Janet jumped from the car and rushed to Jean's side.

"Do you think you've found Ying Mee's treasure?" Janet asked excitedly.

The girls began to dig with their heels. When this proved too hard, Louise ran back to the car and brought out the shovel they always carried with them. Frantically she turned up the earth, making the hole deeper and deeper. Presently a rusty wire was uncovered, and Louise dug farther.

Suddenly the girls' faces fell. Then they burst into laughter.

"It's only the broken rib of an umbrella!" Janet cried out.

"Well, we were warned by Mr. Fish," Louise said, shaking her head. "The metal detector will indicate any kind of metal, valuable or not."

Louise shovelled the dirt back into the hole and tamped it. Then the girls returned to the car.

"Suppose I take a turn with the detector," Janet offered.

She began walking along the road, Louise and Jean following in the car. Now and then another automobile would pass them and its passengers would smile broadly. Apparently they were used to seeing amateur treasure hunters in Mother Lode country.

Janet had walked about half a mile without hearing any pings or humming sounds over the earphones when Louise spotted a stalwart Digger pine tree a little distance ahead. "This tree is very plentiful in this area," she said as Janet got into the car. "I wonder how it came to be called Digger pine."

"It was named after the Digger Indians who used the cones for food," Janet explained. "Sometimes it's called the grey pine."

"Say! Remember Ying Mee's love of trees?" Jean broke in. "I'm sure that tree must have been standing here for a couple of hundred years. Maybe he buried the nuggets under it."

The girls quickly parked and hurried toward the pine. Janet, using the detector, began to circle the huge trunk. Suddenly she called out, "Something here!"

The Danas dashed to join her, Jean swinging the

shovel. Janet pointed out the exact spot where the sounds were loudest and Jean began to dig. It was hard work and presently she said, "I'm beginning to feel like a Digger Indian!"

In a few minutes the girls' search was rewarded. They uncovered a small metal box and eagerly opened it. The treasure inside was not the one for which they were hunting, but the contents, a collection of coins, represented many dollars.

"They're old coins!" Louise said, picking up a couple. "These are both marked 1865."

The entire collection proved to have been coins minted around that date. Janet grinned. "Not bad, eh, for an amateur?"

"You go to the head of the class," Jean replied. "What shall we do with these?"

Louise said she felt sure that along this road any money found was "finders keepers," so the girls divided the coins evenly among themselves.

"I'll treat you all to a meal in Volcano," Janet offered enthusiastically.

Louise and Jean were delighted to see their friend happy once more. Apparently Janet was so sure the police in the Hawaiian Islands would find Major Williams that she had temporarily ceased to worry about him.

"Let's have lunch at Sacramento and dinner in Volcano," Louise proposed.

The others agreed. They kept at their metal-detecting job until they were no longer in the country, then drove directly to the Reed home. When the girls came into the house, Aunt Carol and Aunt Harriet were amazed to see them.

"Are you all right?" the two women asked together.

"We're fine—but starved," Jean said with a grin. "How's the food situation in the Reed restaurant?"

"Give me twenty minutes and I'll serve you a feast fit for a king," Aunt Carol said gaily.

During the delicious meal which followed, the girls brought the two women up to date on all the details of the mysteries.

"Actually we haven't accomplished much," Louise said ruefully. "But it's just possible that the police will catch Basil Tripley and find out whether or not he's the thief—which means I may get back my lovely star sapphire ring."

"I'm sure you will," said Aunt Harriet. She turned to Janet. "These nieces of mine never give up until they've solved their cases."

The three girls left their old coins at the Reed home, and started back directly after luncheon. When they reached the country area once more, they took turns walking along the road with the metal detector. They worked for a couple of hours, but had no luck, and finally gave up. When they reached Sutter Creek, Louise, who was now driving, took the road to Volcano.

"I suppose we don't dare get out of the car after our promise to the police," Jean remarked.

"No. We'll have to search along this road with our metal detector another time," Louise agreed.

She drove on until they reached the Jug and Rose Tearoom, and parked. As they walked inside, Mrs. Thebaut greeted them affably and said:

"Oh, I'm so glad you came. The police have been asking for you."

Janet looked startled. "Oh, dear!" she said worriedly. "We haven't done anything wrong! I'm sure it's all right for us to keep those coins!"

Mrs. Thebaut smiled. "Coins?" she said, a twinkle in her eyes. "What have you girls been up to?"

Janet poured out the whole story. Mrs. Thebaut waited until she had finished, then said, "I doubt that the Jackson police would know anything about those coins yet. Anyway, it's perfectly all right for you to keep them."

"Why do the police want us?" Jean asked.

"I have no idea," Mrs. Thebaut replied. "But do call up the chief in Jackson immediately."

Louise did this. As soon as she had identified herself, her brow puckered. Presently she said, "Yes, we'll come. Do you want us right away, or would it be all right if we have dinner first? . . . Oh, thank you very much. We should be there by seven-thirty."

As Louise hung up the phone and came to the table where Jean, Janet, and Mrs. Thebaut were anxiously waiting, she said, "Guess what! The police may have found Basil Tripley!"

"Really?" Janet exclaimed.

Louise explained that a man fitting his description had been picked up in the woods. He denied being Basil Tripley and the police chief wanted the girls to come to the jail and see if indeed he were the man suspected of stealing Louise's sapphire ring.

Quickly Louise explained to Mrs. Thebaut why they had suspected the mysterious man in the woods, and how they had reported him to the police. The woman smiled at them admiringly. "You are real sleuths," she said. "Well, since you have a date at police headquarters, and you want some dinner, I'd better get busy."

"Anything you have ready will be fine," said Louise.

The three girls were excited, but thoroughly enjoyed the tasty meal. As soon as they had finished, they said good-by and hurried off to Jackson.

The police chief was waiting for them and took the girls to a cell where a man sat on a cot, his head cupped in his hands. Hearing the visitors' footsteps, he looked up.

"Basil Tripley!" Louise cried out. "What did you do with my star sapphire ring?"

The man on the cot had jumped up. His startled glance seemed like a complete giveaway. He paced back and forth a couple of times, then turned and said:

"All right. I'm Basil Tripley. But that doesn't mean a thing. These phony charges of my being a thief and throwing tree limbs and rocks are crazy! You have no proof of anything against me. I'm going to sue you all for keeping me in jail!"

"Calm down!" the police chief said firmly. "I think we have enough evidence against you to hold you here. I've communicated with the San Francisco Police. When I hear from them I'll decide what to do."

Basil Tripley's eyes flashed angrily as he glared at Louise and Jean. "You meddlesome girls! You're responsible for this! I tell you I'm innocent. I *was* in the woods, and incidentally I learned something of great importance there."

"Great importance to whom?" the chief asked.

"To these girls!" Tripley replied.

## CHAPTER XVII

# A Prisoner Bargains

THE GIRLS waited for Basil Tripley to continue, and tell what he claimed to know that was of great importance to them. The prisoner did not say another word.

Finally Jean demanded, "What is this information you've learned?"

Tripley gave a sneering smile. "What do you think I am, anyway, giving you a valuable secret without getting anything in return?"

Suddenly his eyes narrowed and he looked through the bars directly at the girls. "I'll make a bargain with you. If you'll drop all the charges against me and let me out of this place a free man, I'll tell you the secret."

Louise and Jean were taken aback by this announcement. But they had no intention of evading the law, even at the risk of not learning something of value to them. Janet, startled, had put her hand over her mouth as if she were afraid of saying something unwise.

Finally Louise said to the prisoner, "We'll think it over."

She turned on her heel and the others followed. When they were back in the main room of police headquarters, she asked the chief whether he thought Tripley was telling the truth.

"No, I don't. And even if he is, I think there'll be some way of your learning the secret without our granting him his release. When word comes from San Francisco, I'll let you know the results."

The girls left headquarters and returned to the motel. There they discussed the whole affair. All were delighted that Tripley had been captured, but still wished they knew his secret.

"Could he possibly know where the Major is?" Janet queried.

"Or have picked up some information about Ying Mee's buried chest of nuggets?" Jean asked.

Louise had been staring into space. Now she said, "I know one thing it might be."

"What?" Jean and Janet chorused.

"It's a long guess but perhaps Basil Tripley, while hiding out, learned that the man with the long white beard and the clean-shaven elderly man with white hair are the same person!"

Janet's eyes opened wide in astonishment. "You

mean the Major might be wearing a false beard?"

Louise nodded. Janet threw herself at the young sleuth and hugged her. "You're a whiz!"

"Why don't we go right down and confront Basil Tripley with that assertion?" Jean suggested.

Louise held up her hand. "Not so fast, eager beaver. I imagine visiting hours are over for jailbirds! Let's go tomorrow."

This was agreed upon, and early the next morning the girls went to the jail. The chief greeted them warmly and let his visitors go back to Tripley's cell themselves.

The prisoner smiled at them hopefully. "So you've changed your minds and are going to withdraw your charges," he crowed.

"Mr. Tripley," said Jean, staring hard at the suspect, "you found out that the long white beard the old man wears is only a false one!"

The prisoner blinked and stepped back a bit. But he remained silent.

"We know who that old man is," Jean said boldly. "And you do too. So you might as well own up."

Instead of replying, Tripley turned his back.

"There's no use pretending," Jean coaxed. Her words fell on deaf ears. No amount of further questioning could elicit any response from the suspect.

At that moment a turnkey came to tell the girls that the period allowed for a visit was over. The three young sleuths returned to the motel, where Janet phoned her mother for news of the Major. Unfortunately, the Hawaiian Islands clue seemed to have petered out—the police there had found no trace of the missing man. Discouraged, Janet returned to the Danas.

"Oh, dear, what shall we do now?" she asked. "Everything looks so hopeless."

"Don't give up," Louise said kindly. "Let's take a trip out to Jackson Gate and down to that stream where we saw the bearded stranger. Maybe he'll show up again."

But when they reached the spot, no one was in sight.

"Maybe he lives in a cabin hidden among the trees," Jean suggested. "Let's try to find some footprints."

Although the three girls searched thoroughly, they could find none. Wind and an occasional shower had blotted out any made by the man at the time the Danas had been there before. They kept looking for a shack for some time but had no success.

"I'm going to try calling," said Janet finally. At the top of her voice she shouted, "Major! Major! This is Janet! Can you hear me?"

There was no answer—just the merest sound of an echo. All three girls took up the cry, but if Major Williams was in the area, he was not letting it be known. Finally the Danas suggested leaving.

"Oh, please, not yet," Janet begged. "I just had a thought. *If* the Major is around, and if he thinks we have left, he may play his harmonica."

The Danas were sure they were not going to find him, but to please Janet they stopped talking and tiptoed around among the trees, bushes, and open stretches. The search proved fruitless, and finally Janet gave up.

The girls returned to their car. As Louise pulled into Jackson a little later, Jean said, "Let's go down to police headquarters and see what they've found out about Basil Tripley."

When the three sleuths arrived they were amazed to learn that the prisoner was gone.

"You didn't release him?" Louise cried out.

The chief smiled. "Indeed not. Officers from San Francisco were here and took Tripley back with them. He's the con man with a record for whom they've been searching.

"The officers feel sure he's the person who took your ring," the chief told Louise. "But they haven't found it yet, and of course Tripley is still denying having taken it. But I hope it turns up."

The girls thanked him and said good-by. They ate a late lunch before returning to the motel. Janet admitted that she felt very tired and said that she was going to take a nap. "You girls do whatever you wish. Don't bother about me."

The Danas knew that Janet was very much disheartened. If only some break would come in connection with the disappearance of Major Williams! The sisters, hoping that a good sleep would help to restore Janet's optimism, agreed to go off alone.

"There's one place we haven't visited that could have been a good hiding place for Ying Mee's treasure," Louise said.

"Where?"

"The great Indian Rock of the old Mi-woks. You know, the place we were told about that was the fabulous community grinding-stone area."

"That's a great idea," said Jean. "Ying Mee certainly would consider that spot permanent enough so his chest of nuggets would be safe."

"Let's go right away!" Louise urged.

The sisters hurried off and headed for Pine Grove. From there, they took the road toward Volcano and presently saw the enormous rock at the foot of a hillside. They parked the car and walked down to the unique spot.

"It's positively weird!" said Jean. "I never saw such a big, flat rock in my life!"

"I read," Louise spoke up, "that right now it's one hundred and sixty feet wide, but there is lots more of it which has been covered by leaf mold."

"And look at those deep holes pitting the whole surface!" Jean exclaimed.

"There are fifteen hundred of those mortars," her sister said. "I forgot to show you a postcard I bought telling all about it. The Mi-wok used rock pestles to grind their food. They loved manzanita berries, acorns, and wild grains and seeds."

The sisters had just set their metal detector on the ground near the edge of the rock when Jean exclaimed, "Look!"

Louise followed her sister's gaze up the slope. Walking toward them was a Mi-wok Indian woman in tribal costume! Behind her came a photographer carrying a camera and tripod.

As the woman reached the rock, she smiled at the girls and said, "This place where my ancestors gathered is fascinating, isn't it?"

"Yes, indeed," the Danas replied.

"The photograph is for a magazine," the Indian explained. "That's why I'm dressed this way."

She wore a deerskin costume—a sort of cape made of two skins, one hanging down the back, the other down the front. They were tied together at the shoulders and fell well below her hips.

Her skirt consisted of two panels, open at the sides and reaching to her ankles, which were adorned with bracelets of beads. She also wore several bracelets on her arms, and necklaces of various colours.

The Indian woman's long black hair was swept

back from her face and hung in two braids over her shoulders. The braids were interwoven with yellow-dyed strips of hide. A few variegated feathers were tucked into her hair at the crown of her head.

"You look very attractive," Louise said admiringly.

The woman thanked her, then seated herself at one of the mortars, her knees flanking it. She held a stone pestle in her hands as the photographer squinted through his finder.

"I wish we had brought our camera," said Louise ruefully.

When the photographer offered to sell them a print, Louise accepted and gave the motel address.

"What did your people eat besides the things they ground in the mortars?" Jean asked the Indian woman.

"Rabbit, squirrel, deer, and fish. Also large insects which were spiced and flavoured."

Jean was sure she would not relish insects in her diet!

"My ancestors got their starch from wild-lily bulbs, particularly the Mariposa, and ate them with roasted grasshoppers, followed by manzanita berry cider."

"The bulbs and cider sound all right," Louise said, smiling.

"My people also ate toyon berries. They come in

clusters of bright red. But you have to get to them before the robins, juncos, and sparrows do!"

"Well," said the photographer, "now that you girls have heard the menu of the old Mi-wok, will you please step out of range of the camera so I can get to work?"

Louise and Jean flushed a bit, made their apologies, and walked away with the metal detector. Louise adjusted the headpiece and held up the detecting apparatus. Slowly the girls began their trek along the edge of the vast rock. There was no sound on the earphones.

"If a lot of this rock has been covered," Louise said, "we ought to move farther out."

By this time the photographer had finished his work and looked up. The Indian woman smiled pleasantly at the girls, but the photographer said with a derisive laugh, "You girls are wasting your time hunting for hidden gold. You'll find no treasure here."

"He's a pest!" Jean muttered.

But an hour later, after the two had gone, she and Louise were ready to admit that the photographer was right. They had found various pieces of metal but nothing of value. On the way back to the motel, neither of them spoke. Both felt too discouraged.

"I hope Janet's in better spirits," said Louise as they reached the motel.

They knocked on her door. There was no answer. They looked around the grounds, then asked the proprietor if she had seen Janet. The woman shook her head.

"Maybe she left us a note," Louise said hopefully, and the girls went to their own room.

But no note was there. Louise and Jean showered, then dressed. Still Janet had not returned.

"Where in the world could she have gone?" Louise asked worriedly.

Dinnertime came and went. Jean and Louise ate fruit and crackers in their room. Still no word from Janet. By this time the girls were becoming alarmed about their friend!

## CHAPTER XVIII

# Flashlight Sleuthing

"I CAN'T stand it another minute!" Jean said. "Don't you think we should go out and look for Janet?"

"Where?" Louise asked.

Jean thought a moment, then said she would run downtown and see if anyone in Jackson had seen Janet. "Why don't you stay here in case she or somebody else phones us?" she proposed.

"All right," Louise agreed. "If anyone *does* phone, I hope it will be *good* news. I'll keep my fingers crossed!"

Jean drove off in the car. When she reached town, she inquired in various restaurants, a few shops which were still open, and finally the hotel. At each place she gave a description of Janet Crane, but no one had seen her.

"Maybe I'd better go to the police," Jean

thought, as she came out onto the hotel porch and walked down the steps to the street.

The young sleuth turned toward headquarters. Just then Jean saw a familiar figure coming along the sidewalk. Tim Salter!

"Hi!" he called cheerfully, when he reached her. "Hey, what do you know? Beauty jumped twenty feet!"

"All at once?" Jean asked, amazed.

Tim grinned. "Come on, now. She's not a kangaroo—she's a frog! But she's pretty good. She did the twenty feet in two jumps."

Jean asked whether the jumping had taken place inside the trough or out of it.

"Outside!" Tim replied proudly. "I'm sure Pa and I are goin' to win that eight-hundred-dollar prize!"

"Well, I sure hope you do," said Jean. "Say, Tim, do you remember the girl who was with my sister and me the day we stopped at your cabin?"

"You mean the one you called Janet?"

"Yes. Have you seen her around?"

"In town you mean?" Tim answered. "No. But I did see her going into the woods."

"When was this?" Jean asked eagerly.

"Oh, about four o'clock, when I was on my way to town. She didn't see me, though."

"Have you any idea where she was heading?"

"No. But she was in a real big hurry. She was almost running."

Jean was puzzled as to how Janet had reached the spot. She asked Tim if he knew.

The boy shook his head. "Maybe somebody drove her there."

"Where was the place you saw Janet going into the woods?" Jean queried him excitedly.

Tim described it. Jean thought, "That's exactly where we entered the woods the day we found the Salters' cabin."

She quickly said good-by to Tim, hurried to her car, and drove to the motel as fast as the speed limit allowed. She relayed her discovery to Louise, then asked, "Have you heard anything?"

"Not a word," her sister replied. "Janet must have picked up some clue and followed it herself. But she's been gone so long, I'm afraid she has run into trouble. We'd better go to the woods and look for her!"

"We'll need another flashlight," said Jean. "Maybe I can borrow one from the proprietor."

She hurried up the stairs and found the woman in the lobby. Jean explained what had happened and was given the additional flashlight.

"Do be careful in those woods, especially at night," the motel owner warned.

"We will, thanks," Jean promised as she dashed out the front door.

Louise had already brought the car up from the parking lot. Her sister jumped in, slammed the door, and they sped off.

"What kind of clue do you think Janet picked up?" Jean asked.

"I've been thinking it over," her sister answered. "Maybe she only had a hunch."

"About what?"

Louise said slowly, "If Janet believes the Major is hiding out in the woods around here, she may have thought there was more chance of tracking him down in the evening."

"Evening?" Jean echoed. "You mean that's when he might be most apt to play his harmonica, and could be traced by the music?"

"That, and the possibility of some well-concealed shack or cabin which could be spotted by lights inside."

"Good hunch, Louise. I hope it pays off."

When the Danas reached the spot where they were going to start their hunt for Janet, they parked well off the road and locked the car. Turning on their flashlights, the young sleuths began to pick their way through the dark woods.

After proceeding a distance, Louise said, "It may help if we start shouting Janet's name."

Jean agreed and the sisters took turns calling loudly. There was no answer.

"I hate to mention it," said Jean, "but we've

been warned so many times about uncovered mine shafts, I'm afraid Janet may have fallen into one of them."

Louise declared she had the same worry, but had tried to shut it out of her mind. After calling out several times and getting no response, they finally gave up. Their fears for Janet's safety mounted.

Nevertheless, the girls trekked on. As they went, Jean said, "I wonder if Pa Salter was in town with his son. I didn't think to ask Tim. If Pa is home, it might be a good idea to stop at his cabin and ask him if he saw Janet."

Louise thought this an excellent idea. "I wonder in what direction the cabin is from here."

Neither girl was sure, but figured that by walking downhill, they should come to the stream which ran past the cabin. Accordingly, they took a downward course and in a few minutes could hear the babbling of the stream.

When they reached it, Jean asked, "Do we go left or right? I'm completely confused. This may not even be the brook we're looking for!"

"I feel positively stupid not to know," Louise answered, "but my hunch is to go to the right."

Jean said, "Okay, let's try it," and the sisters set off in that direction. They walked for some distance without coming to the cabin.

"I was hoping there'd be a light in it," said

Louise. "But I presume there won't be any if nobody's home."

The girls trudged on. Several minutes later Jean was just about to propose that they turn back when a large object loomed up indistinctly in the distance. They proceeded toward it.

A cabin!

Louise, playing the beam of her flashlight around, picked up the trough in which Beauty was being trained to jump. "This is the Salters' cabin," she said. "But it's dark. Nobody home."

The sisters felt completely stymied in their efforts. They discussed what they should do now.

Finally Louise suggested that Pa Salter might be inside asleep. "Shall we pound on the door and find out?"

"We'd better not do that," her sister advised. "It might frighten him. Tell you what: Why don't we just shine a light through the window quickly and find out if he's at home? Then we'll awaken him without a scare."

The cabin had a front and back door, and five windows. The first room into which the girls beamed their lights and peered was the kitchen. No one was there.

They moved to a side window and flashed their lights inside. This proved to be the main room of the two-room cabin. There were three cots within.

"Oh!" Jean gasped.

*On one cot lay the white-bearded man, fast asleep!*

"The old man we've been looking for!" Louise exclaimed.

The girls put out their lights and stepped back a little distance. In whispers they discussed the situation.

"Pa Salter gave us the impression that he hadn't seen this man," said Jean. "Do you suppose he lives here or has just helped himself to the cabin?"

"If you'll recall exactly what Pa Salter said," Louise reminded her sister, "it was 'I can't tell you anything about the older man.'"

"Yes, I remember that. Then the Salters must be hiding him!" Jean whispered. "I guess we'd better leave the poor man alone."

Louise disagreed. She reminded her sister that after all their mission was to find Janet. "I think we should wake up the old man and question him," she said.

Once more she shone her light through the window. Jean had run to the front door to knock on it. But this was not necessary. The white-bearded stranger had already been aroused. He sat up on the cot, a look of fright in his eyes. The next moment he stood up and ran to the kitchen, closing the door behind him.

"He's going to run away again!" Jean whispered.

Louise nodded. "Go stand near the front door, in case he comes out, while I go to the back," Louise told her sister.

Though she herself got to the rear of the cabin in plenty of time to stop the stranger before he might come outside, he did not emerge. Louise shone her light through the kitchen window. The man was not in sight!

"We want to talk to you, sir!" Louise cried in a loud voice. "It's very important! Please let us in!"

There was no reply to her pleading.

Assuming that the man had returned to the living room, Louise once more ran to the side of the house and shone her light inside. He was not there!

Jean, in the meantime, realizing from her sister's cries that the man was still inside the cabin, now joined Louise. "Where could he have gone?" she asked.

"I can't think of anything but a cellar," Louise answered.

A look of determination came over Jean's face. "If either door is unlocked, I'm going inside and find that old man!"

The kitchen door was not locked and she went in. Almost at once her flashlight revealed a trap door in the floor. By this time, Louise had joined her sister.

"He's probably hiding down there," Jean whispered.

She lifted the trap door and shone her flashlight below. The girls gaped in astonishment. Instead of a cellar there was just a dirt incline. No one was in sight.

"Let's see where this goes," Louise proposed, and the girls started down the incline.

The dirt and rock opening proved to be a tunnel, which the girls guessed had once been a narrow horizontal shaft to a mine.

They shone their flashlights ahead and proceeded cautiously. The old man had vanished.

Louise and Jean hurried on, calling constantly that they intended no harm—they just wanted to talk to the white-bearded man. Only the eerie echoes of their own voices reached the girls' ears.

Nevertheless, the sisters trudged on.

## CHAPTER XIX

# A Dangerous Plunge

THE TUNNEL leading from the Salter cabin was dark and still.

"I wonder where it goes," said Louise.

"Probably to the water," Jean guessed.

In a few seconds the girls came to the last few yards which turned sharply upward. Brush had been laid over the exit.

Quickly the Danas pushed the briers aside. They found themselves near the bank of the stream.

To their disappointment, the white-bearded stranger was still not in sight!

"He couldn't have gone far," said Louise. "Let's try to find him."

The two girls played their flashlights up and down the stream and among the trees and bushes. Still they caught no sight of the stranger.

"Surely he can't be far away," Jean insisted. "Let's look behind every tree in this area."

They started a systematic search which was rewarded a few minutes later. In the glare of their lights Louise and Jean found their quarry. He was standing behind a large oak. He stared at the girls but said nothing.

Louise and Jean smiled at him. "Why did you run away?" Louise asked gently. "We do not intend any harm. Please believe us. We just want to talk to you."

The old man finally spoke. "Who are you?"

He was tall, slender, and stood very straight. His face held great composure, although his eyes seemed sad.

Louise stepped closer and looked directly at him. Smiling, she said, "We're friends of your granddaughter, Janet Crane. You *are* Major Williams, aren't you?"

The man did not reply. He merely shifted uncomfortably.

With a twinkle in her eyes, Jean asked, "That beard you're wearing is a false one, isn't it?"

A startled look came over the stranger's face. Finally he spoke. "It doesn't matter who I am," he said in a low tone. "I just want to be left alone."

The Danas were not discouraged by this response. Louise went on, "You ran away from the rest home because you thought you were no longer welcome at your daughter's. You decided you were not going to be asked to return there. Isn't that true?"

The white-bearded man looked down at the ground and sighed, but did not reply.

Jean went on with the story. "It's not true that your daughter and your granddaughter don't want you at home. As a matter of fact, they're frantic because they don't know where you are."

The stranger raised his eyes and blinked. They glistened as if tears were forming.

Louise decided it was time to put forth her most persuasive argument. "Major Williams, your granddaughter Janet has been up here in Mother Lode country with us hunting for you.

"Tonight she disappeared in these woods without telling us she was going," Louise went on. "We believe Janet came here because she picked up some clue to your whereabouts. Anyhow, we've been looking for her everywhere with no luck."

"We're really alarmed," Jean added. "She—she may have fallen into an old mine shaft!"

As if roused from a dream, the white-bearded man suddenly pulled off his whiskers. "Yes," he said, "I am Major Williams. All you say about the ideas I had is true. I don't know who you are, but if you're telling the truth about my daughter's

wanting me back, this is one of the happiest moments of my life."

The Danas introduced themselves, then he went
on, "But what's this about Janet being lost?
Were you just telling me that to force me to reveal
my identity?"

Louise and Jean shook their heads vigorously.
"Indeed we weren't, Major Williams," Jean insisted. "We are positive Janet came into these
woods hunting for you," Louise told him ear-
nestly. "Besides searching, we've called and called,
but she doesn't answer."

The Major buried his face in his hands. "Oh, if
anything has happened to Janet, I'm the one to
blame! We must save her!"

At that moment the three were startled to hear
someone crashing through the bushes. The next
instant a light could be seen bobbing toward them.

The newcomer proved to be Pa Salter. He
stared in utter astonishment at the group.

Blinking, he asked, "What's going on here?"

"Your secret is out, Mr. Salter," said Jean.
"When we were here before asking you about two
old men, you knew the truth the whole time!"

Pa Salter grinned. "I was only obeying instruc-
tions," he declared. "The Major here wanted to
board at our cabin secretly. I didn't even tell him
you three girls were here. Well, have you solved
your mystery yet?"

"We've solved two mysteries," Louise told him. "That young man who came here asking for us is now in jail," she announced.

"Jail!" Pa Salter cried out. "Why?"

Very briefly Louise gave an account of Basil Tripley, then went on, "And now the mystery of locating Major Williams is solved too. But I have no idea how much you know of *his* secret."

Major Williams confessed that he had confided little. He admitted having told Pa Salter he was prospecting and hunting for an ancient treasure.

"But I didn't say I had run away—that seemed too much like what a small boy might do."

Pa Salter laughed and slapped his thigh. "Well, that's a good one," he said.

The Major seemed disinclined to reveal any more of his family problems, so the Danas said nothing on the subject. They now told Mr. Salter of their great worry about their friend Janet Crane.

"I met your son Tim in town," Jean revealed. "He said he had seen her come into the woods late this afternoon."

"And you're afraid she's lost?" the man questioned. "This is a bad place for a stranger to get lost."

Before Jean had a chance to reply, another figure with a flashlight hurried toward them. It was Tim Salter, who looked in astonishment at the group. Then he asked the Danas, "Where's your friend Janet?"

After the girl's disappearance had been explained, the Danas urged a search by all of them.

Louise turned to Major Williams. "Do you feel equal to it?" she asked. "Or would you rather stay here?"

"No, indeed, I want to go," the ex-Army man said stanchly. "Life in the open has restored my health completely. Come on! We *must* find my granddaughter!"

Treading carefully as they went, the group spread out in a line. They carefully scrutinized every spot that might conceal a mine opening. During the whole time they kept calling Janet's name.

A full half hour went by before the Danas and their companions suddenly picked up a clue. It came in the form of a faraway voice. Everyone stopped to listen intently.

"There it is!" Jean whispered.

Muffled and indistinct, yet definite, came a cry, "Help! Help!"

"Say! That sounds like it might be coming from underground," Pa Salter observed.

"But *where?*" Louise asked, puzzled.

"Don't know yet, but let's keep followin' the voice," Pa Salter advised, and the line of searchers moved forward.

"Janet! Janet!" Louise and Jean yelled together at the top of their lungs.

"Help! Help!" came the reply, somewhat louder.

"We're getting closer!" Jean cried excitedly.

Suddenly Louise called out, "Stop! Here's a big hole!"

The others rushed to her side. Before them yawned the black opening of a cave-in.

"A deserted mine shaft!" Jean exclaimed.

"Help! Help me!" came a pleading cry from its depths.

"Janet! Are you down there?" Jean called loudly.

"Yes! Oh, thank goodness you've come! Get me out of here!"

Louise and Jean had advanced to the very edge of the old mine shaft. Louise knelt down.

"Here's a flashlight for you. Catch!" She tossed it down to the imprisoned girl.

At that instant the edge of the mine shaft suddenly began to move and crumble rapidly beneath the Danas! Louise and Jean tried to jump back to safety, but to no avail. The earth literally fell away under their feet.

The next moment the two sisters pitched forward and downward into the yawning chasm!

# CHAPTER XX

# The Gold Rocker

AT THE top of the mine shaft Major Williams stood speechless with terror. Pa Salter and his son Tim, fearful Louise and Jean had been injured, went into action immediately. Mr. Salter ordered the others back from the hole. He himself grabbed a tree, and leaning far forward, shone his flashlight down the gaping hole.

The pit was about twenty feet deep. The Dana sisters were just picking themselves up. Janet Crane was standing—proof that she had not been injured in her fall onto the soft earth.

"They're all right!" Pa Salter reported.

"Thank goodness!" Major Williams gasped. "But we must get them out right away!"

The Salters offered to dash back to their cabin and bring a long coil of rope. They hurried off.

At the bottom of the old mine shaft Louise was saying to Janet, "Oh, we were so frightened about you! But before you tell us what happened, we have some marvellous news for you. The Major is here—right up above you!"

"What!" Janet cried incredulously.

The happy girl could hardly believe the good news, as Louise and Jean related the full story. "You girls are simply terrific sleuths!" she squealed, hugging them both.

"You're a full-fledged detective yourself," Jean told her friend. "If you hadn't come to the woods this evening, who knows if or when the Major would've been found."

"But why did you go off without leaving any word?" Louise asked Janet.

She replied that Hep Delaney had come to the motel and insisted that the harmonica player in the woods could be found in a little cabin along a stream. Although somewhat dubious, Janet had decided to take the chance and investigate.

"That practical joker gave me a ride out here— wouldn't even wait until I wrote a note—then left me here.

"From the way Hep described the place, I figured it was somewhere beyond the Salters' cabin," Janet went on. "I guess I just got too excited about my search, and didn't look where I was going. The next thing I knew the brush covering on this old mine shaft gave way and down I went. I tried and tried to climb out, but it was useless.

Oh, girls, is my grandfather really up there?"

"Major Williams," Jean called, "say something to Janet. She doesn't believe you've been found!"

"Yes, I'm really here, Janet dear, and glad of it," the Major replied. "While we're waiting for you to be rescued, I'll tell you my story."

The girls below listened with rapt attention as Major Williams began his account. He said he had become interested in the Mother Lode country and the ancient Lemurians who reputedly had buried gold there. Convinced by certain busybodies at the nursing home that he was no longer welcome at his daughter's, he had decided to make a search in Amador County.

"I had money with me because after I lost heavily in the stock market six months ago, I decided to keep what I had left in cash." Chuckling, he added that, knowing his daughter would not approve, he had not told her.

"I used to go down to Angels Camp to the annual frog-jumping contests," Major Williams explained. "One time I met the Salters there. They told me where their cabin was and I decided to hide out here and make it my headquarters.

"After I left the rest home, I went to a store in San Francisco and purchased a harmonica to play when I felt lonely. I also bought a beard to use as a disguise. Then I took a bus to Sacramento, and hitchhiked from there to this area."

Janet called up, "It was the Danas who guessed you had a harmonica and wore a false beard, Major. But you didn't wear it all the time, I suppose. The woman and children who saw a man trying to steal your harmonica in the woods said you had no beard."

"That's right," her grandfather replied. "The young rascal found out my beard disguise and that my harmonica is a valuable one. He said he wanted it for two reasons: to 'shut some people up'—I assume he meant to stop you girls from getting a clue to me—and also he could sell the instrument."

Suddenly the Danas began to laugh. "Now we know what Basil Tripley's bargaining information was!" said Louise. She told Major Williams that the man was now in jail, and had tried to bargain his way out.

At that moment the Salters returned with the rope. One end was tied securely around the tree near the edge of the hole, the other was lowered to the girls.

"You go first," the Danas urged Janet.

She needed no further urging. Nimbly the joyful girl went hand over hand up the rope and in a few moments was in her grandfather's arms.

"Oh, Major! Major! How good to see you again!" she sobbed as he hugged her warmly.

As soon as Louise and Jean were safely above-ground, the Salters invited the whole group to come to their cabin to clean up a bit and have hot soup and sandwiches.

"We accept!" Janet said for the bedraggled girls, and they set off.

At the cabin everyone enjoyed the appetizing snack. During it the barest details of Major Williams' secret were divulged to the Salters. He paid them for his lodging, then packed his few belongings. Good-bys were said, and the Danas led the way to the car.

When they reached the motel, Janet introduced Major Williams, who registered for a room near the girls. But before going to the lower level, Janet insisted that the others wait for her while she put in a telephone call to her mother.

Mrs. Crane was overwhelmed at the news. "What a joyous surprise!" she exclaimed. "It hardly seems true. Please put Father on the wire right away!"

A lengthy conversation followed between Major Williams and his daughter. All the sadness left his eyes and Mrs. Crane's buoyant voice sounded like that of a schoolgirl.

"I'll drive up tomorrow to get you and Janet," she said happily. "Oh, this will be a marvellous reunion!"

Major Williams, though still talking into the telephone, looked directly at the sisters. "There's one thing we must never forget—our gratitude to the Dana girls."

Louise and Jean smiled, saying it was a great privilege for them to have helped solve the case. As soon as Major Williams and his daughter finished talking, the young sleuths telephoned to Aunt Harriet and Aunt Carol.

"You solved the case!" Aunt Harriet exclaimed, after Jean had given her the news.

"But we haven't solved our other mystery," Jean went on. "Louise and I want to stay here a little longer and see if we can't wind that one up too."

Miss Dana said she had just received some very good news too, and asked to speak to Louise. "The police have just called here to say that your sapphire ring has been found!"

"Oh, I'm so happy!" Louise cried out. "Where?"

Aunt Harriet said that the police had finally obtained a full confession from Basil Tripley. They had investigated a small flat which he rented and had found it there, along with a great deal of other stolen valuables.

"Did Basil Tripley say why he was up in Mother Lode country?" Louise asked.

"Yes. You girls were right about that. Actually he was eavesdropping on us in Sacramento because of your conversation on the plane, and learned our secret. He trailed you here, hoping you would locate the chest of nuggets. Then he planned to steal it."

Miss Dana went on to say that Tripley had not tried to harm the girls until he realized they definitely suspected he was the ring thief. Then he had broken off the dead tree limb and hurled it toward them. Later, he had tossed the big rock and the warning note.

After the phone call was over, and the Danas and their friends were seated in the sisters' room discussing the whole case, Janet said, "Louise and Jean, I feel very bad that your Aunt Carol's mystery has not been solved."

"Another mystery?" Major Williams asked in amazement.

Quickly the Danas told him about the chest of nuggets buried by their ancestor's Chinese servant Ying Mee. "I'm almost beginning to think it's hopeless trying to locate it," Louise admitted with a sigh.

Jean listed all the clues they had picked up and the places where they had looked.

The Major was thoughtful for several moments. Then he spoke up. "You say Ying Mee was a great admirer of beautiful trees?"

"Yes," Louise answered.

"It's just possible—oh, very vaguely possible— that I might have a clue for you," Major Williams said, a twinkle in his eyes.

The three girls looked at him in astonishment. He went on, "You also said you used the metal detector at Indian Rock? Did you happen to notice an ancient water oak out there?"

The girls confessed they had not. "Well," the Major continued, "I understand it's one of the oldest, most ruggedly handsome of these trees in the state. One day, when I was over in that area, the oak fascinated me, so I went to have a closer look at it. Beneath its giant limbs was a good-sized rock. Most of it was underground, but I wondered if it might be a clue to my Lemurian cave, so I decided to dig down and unearth it. Carved on the underside of the rock were several Chinese characters."

"Chinese characters!" Jean repeated. "Do you know what they said?"

"No, I don't. I figured possibly some Chinese had been buried there, and this was his grave marker. But I couldn't figure out why, if this were true, the characters had been put on the underside."

Louise and Jean were excited. "You think now that possibly this rock was a marker for our chest of nuggets?" Louise asked.

Major Williams chuckled. "It's a very slim clue, but I think it's worth investigating, don't you?"

"I most certainly do!" Jean answered. "How about all of us going over there right now?"

A second later she rescinded her suggestion, realizing what a physical and emotional strain Major Williams and his granddaughter had been under.

"We'd love to go with you and Louise first thing tomorrow morning!" Janet offered eagerly, and the Major nodded.

The whole group said good night and went to bed immediately. But they were up for an early breakfast, and set out in high spirits for the Indian Grinding Grounds. When they reached it, the car was parked and the treasure hunters, carrying their digging equipment and the metal detector, hastened across the grassy slope to the old water oak which Major Williams indicated.

"This is the rock." He pointed to the one he had unearthed a few weeks before.

"Here's hoping!" Jean exclaimed, as she and the others began shovelling.

The soil around the boulder was fairly soft and the diggers had no difficulty making headway. They were careful to leave enough earth surrounding the rock to prevent its slipping. Presently the Chinese characters were revealed.

Feverishly the girls went on digging below the rock. Two feet of soil had been removed when they struck something hard. The dirt flew faster.

"There must be another rock under here," Janet spoke up breathlessly.

"No—it's not a rock!" Jean exclaimed. "It's something metallic!"

In less than a minute the girls had dug away the soil from the metal object. It was rectangular in shape—about eight inches long, six inches wide, and three inches deep.

"A chest!" Louise's hands were actually trembling with excitement as she knelt and lifted the small chest from the hole. She placed it on solid ground. Together she and Jean forced open the rusted lid.

"Nuggets!" Janet cried out.

"Oh, do you suppose this is our family treasure?" Jean asked tensely.

Silently but quickly the Danas took out each nugget. At the very bottom of the chest Louise discovered an unusual-looking one.

"A rocker!" Major Williams exclaimed.

Louise and Jean looked at each other. "It's ours —really ours!" Jean said, almost sobbing with delight.

Louise had bowed her head to hide sudden tears. Thoughts of faithful old Ying Mee having buried this gold for the use of the Reed family swept over her. She could not speak at once.

But finally the girls and Major Williams began talking joyously at the same time.

"We can never thank you enough for your wonderful clue," Jean declared to the elderly man.

He, in turn, said he never could adequately repay the Danas for their efforts in reuniting him with his family.

"Nor I," said Janet warmly. "And I know that Mother feels the same way."

Dirt was shovelled back into the hole and the group walked solemnly but happily back to their car. After an excited phone call to Aunt Carol, and a celebration luncheon in Jackson, they returned to the motel to pack their clothes.

While waiting for Mrs. Crane to arrive, the Danas and their friends sat on the patio, discussing the mysteries from beginning to end.

Suddenly Jean began to giggle. "There's one little score in this town which I'd like to settle before we leave," she said. "Excuse me a minute, please."

She went up to the telephone in the lobby and called up Hep Delaney. He answered promptly.

In as sweet a voice as she could muster, Jean said, "Oh, Hep, thanks so much for giving us a good clue to the harmonica player."

The boy began to laugh uproariously. "Janet fell for that, all right. Nifty trick, eh?"

When he subsided, Jean went on, "Will you do me a big favour, Hep? Bring your harmonica up to the motel and play for us?"

Hep seemed nonplused by the invitation. "You think I can't play, eh?" he said. "Well, I'll show you. I'll be there in about ten minutes. You're going to hear some *real* harmonica playing!"

Jean was grinning broadly as she descended the steps to the garden. When she reached the group, she said, "Major Williams, would you do something for me, please? Put on your beard and get your harmonica. Later on, if you feel like playing for us, will you do so?"

"Be glad to."

Jean did not explain further, and the other girls looked at her with twinkling eyes.

"Jean has some joke percolating!" Louise thought.

Major Williams, wearing the false beard, had just returned with his harmonica in a pocket when a truck roared down the driveway, pulled into the parking lot, and stopped with a screech of brakes. Hep Delaney jumped out and walked toward the Danas and their friends. He was introduced to Major Williams.

"So you want to hear the best harmonica player in Amador County, eh?" Hep bragged, pulling a harmonica of medium size from his pocket.

Tilting his head upward and adjusting his hands, he began to play. Hep finished an old-time jig which had many off-key notes sprinkled throughout the melody.

"Have you finished?" Jean asked, applauding. Then she said, "It really takes the high school crowd to play the harmonica, don't you think, Hep?"

"Sure does," the youth agreed. He promptly began a modern tune, which was so discordant in places that it sent chills up and down the listeners' backs.

By this time Major Williams had caught on to the fact that Jean was trying to teach this young braggart a lesson. Although he was entirely unaware that it was because of himself, he was glad to play the game.

Taking out his own harmonica, he said with a laugh, "You know, Hep, I used to play this a lot when I was your age. Wonder what I can do now."

Hep Delaney looked scornful. Rudely he put his hands over his ears and made a wry face. Then he shrugged. "Okay, old boy. Let's see what you can do!"

Major Williams gave an amused smile, then began to play. How beautiful the melody was! Not one sour note. The piece became more and more intricate, and even before he finished playing it, Janet and the Danas began to clap enthusiastically.

"Just wonderful!" Louise said.

Everyone suddenly glanced at Hep. His expression had changed from derision to complete astonishment. Then, without a word, he shuffled away from the group and went to his car. He hoisted himself inside, started the motor, and disappeared up the driveway.

The others burst into laughter. "That'll teach him!" Janet giggled. "Wonderful idea, Jean!"

Louise smiled, then asked softly, "Major Williams, please play some more."

Little did Louise and Jean know as they listened to the delightful music that in a short time they would be involved in another exciting mystery, *The Secret of Lost Lake*.

On the following pages you will find details of other exciting books from Sparrow.

# MYSTERY OF THE STONE TIGER

## Carolyn Keene

*Dana Girls Mystery No. 1: A series from the author of the Nancy Drew Books.*

A black-robed ghost stalks the streets of Oak Falls . . .

A tiger roams the woods on the outskirts of town . . .

The Hilary Museum is haunted by a phantom prowler who passes through locked doors and bolted windows. The police are baffled and the whole town is frightened. In desperation, Elise Hilary begs the Dana girls to solve the awful mystery surrounding her museum. Determined to unravel the eerie puzzle, Louise and Jean Dana take on the job and involve themselves in a series of frightening adventures as they follow a twisting maze of clues to find the solution of this exciting mystery.

95p

# THE RIDDLE OF THE FROZEN FOUNTAIN

## Carolyn Keene

*Dana Girls Mystery No. 2: A series from the author of the Nancy Drew books.*

Mysteries have a way of finding the Dana girls, no matter where they are. This time it all begins when Professor Crandall of Starhurst School receives an anonymous note, warning him not to remove the valuable bronze fountain that he has just purchased from an estate nearby. Louise and Jean courageously set out to track down the writer of the threatening note – and in doing so become deeply enmeshed in a series of bizarre and baffling events, including the midnight appearance of phantom ice skaters on the school pond.

95p

# THE SECRET OF THE SILVER DOLPHIN

## Carolyn Keene

*Dana Girls Mystery no. 3: A series from the author of the Nancy Drew Books.*

Judy Platt is desperately trying to find the silver dolphin mentioned in her dead brother's will – but no one knows whether the lost dolphin is a live mammal or a silver ornament. When Louise and Jean Dana hear a newscast announcing a reward to anyone who can locate the dolphin, they immediately take up the challenge to solve the strange mystery.

Their dangerous quest for the mysterious dolphin leads them to a deserted Caribbean island where they find themselves caught up in one of the most exciting and baffling adventures they have ever faced.

95p